The Space We're In

The Space We're In

Katya Balen

MARGARET FERGUSON BOOKS
HOLIDAY HOUSE · NEW YORK
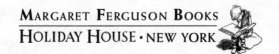

Margaret Ferguson Books

Copyright © Katya Balen

HOLIDAY HOUSE is registered in the U.S. Patent and Trademark Office.

Printed and bound in August 2019 at Maple Press, York, PA, USA.

www.holidayhouse.com

The Space We're In was first published in Great Britain by
Bloomsbury, 2019, in a somewhat different form.

First Edition, 2019

1 3 5 7 9 10 8 6 4 2

Photo of *Mona Lisa* from illustrated Encyclopedia "Treasures of art",
Partnership «Prosvesheniye», St. Petersburg, Russia, 1906 / Shutterstock
Photo of spiral galaxy ESA-Hubble / Shutterstock

Library of Congress Cataloging-in-Publication Data

Names: Balen, Katya, author.
Title: The space we're in / Katya Balen.
Other titles: Space we are in
Description: New York : Margaret Ferguson Books, Holiday House, [2019] |
Summary: Ten-year-old Frank's life revolves around his autistic brother,
five-year-old Max, but after many changes over the course of a year, he
discovers that he loves Max and is proud of him.
Identifiers: LCCN 2018057418 | ISBN 9780823442898 (hardcover)
Subjects: | CYAC: Brothers—Fiction. | Autism—Fiction. | Family
life—England—Fiction. | Schools—Fiction. | Friendship—Fiction. |
England—Fiction.
Classification: LCC PZ7.1.B3573 Sp 2019 | DDC [Fic]—dc23
LC record available at https://lccn.loc.gov/2018057418

For my parents, and for Patrick

The Space We're In

In the spiral cipher code, the first time you use a letter in your message it starts as one number but changes each time you use it. So A=1, B=2 the first time; the second time, A=30, B=31, and so forth. This diagram ends at 58 but the spiral keeps going, depending on the number of repeated letters you use in your message.

13 5 12 20 4 15 23 14

I AM TEN and Max is five. There are twenty-six days until Max starts school and we're going to buy new shoes for the new school. We've looked at his special hard plastic book with its little Velcro-y laminated pictures of all his favorite things and the ones that show him what's happening now and next. It has a blue silky-smooth strap so he can wear it around his neck when we're not at home and he needs to know what's going to happen. He doesn't like the weight and the click-clack of the plastic pages though so Mum carries it for him instead. Mum showed him the picture for shoe store and we whirled around the world on Google Street View trying to find the store to show him so he's prepared but it's not there so she's worried worried worried. I went to Egypt on Google Street View and I showed Max but he was jumping up and down so he didn't get to look at the pyramids. Now we are in the car. *New shoes new school* Mum says to Max. Max doesn't say anything because he never says anything and he doesn't stop humming even though I ask him to stop humming.

I'm not going to a new school but I'm getting new shoes. I think that might be confusing Max, so I tell him that I'm not going to a new school. *You are* I say. *You're going to a new school.* Max keeps humming. I tell him to shut up and Mum doesn't say *don't tell your brother to shut up, Frank* because she's worried about the new shoes new school.

We get to the shoe store and Mum parks the car too close to a wall so I have to wait in my seat while she gets Max out. She puts his reins on and I say *giddyup* but she doesn't laugh. Max flaps his hands and Mum shows him his special book and I say *new shoes!* but Max doesn't like that. Mum tells him words using her hands, she says *new* and she says *first shoes, then cookie* but Max isn't looking so he can't listen.

We go into the store and Max is still humming so people look at him. I used to tell people he was talking but I don't say that anymore. The store is big, too big for Max. I don't see anyone I know and that makes me happy but it's not the sort of happy that makes me smile. I go and look at cool shoes with high tops and long laces and I hold a pair up and Mum doesn't say no because she's telling the shoe lady that she can't touch Max's feet but that Mum thinks they're a size two. The lady says she'd like to measure Max's feet because they don't like to sell shoes that don't fit and wouldn't it be easier not to have to bring them back?

Mum smiles but she's not smiling really, and says that she just wants the same shoes Max is wearing but bigger and if we have to come back we will just come back.

Max is humming louder and louder and his hands are flapping down by his sides and not up in the air like he does when he's happy so I think we might have to go. Mum talks to Max with her hands and gives him a ball to squish with his hands because that might stop them flapping.

The shoe lady isn't happy and says to Max to come here so she can have a little look-see at his feet. I want to tell her to shut up but I don't want to say anything at all so I just keep looking at the shoes with high tops and I choose ones with blue laces. I pick them up and check the size and it's perfect for me. The shoe store lady says *lots of little boys don't like having their feet measured* and she's *sure he'll be fine* and that *he's a brave boy and there are stickers for brave boys* and *does he like soccer* because she has soccer stickers and *does he play soccer or support a soccer team or perhaps he likes Match Attax cards because little boys like those a lot, don't they?* And then it's too many words and Max is having his meltdown.

I don't know why they call it that because when something like ice melts it pours itself into a puddle and it isn't hard anymore. When Max melts he's the hardest thing in the world and you think he's going to explode his bones from his body. He bites and bites and bites at his fists and his humming is a scream from his chest and nose and mouth. He is fury and he's lost himself and everyone and everything and everywhere.

All the people in the store are looking at the furious biting boy even though they're grown-ups and it's rude to stare and the store lady doesn't say anything anymore. Mum is using her hands again to say *finished finished finished* and she says it with her mouth too. She picks Max up because he is stiff and small and not a puddle but he kicks and lashes and twists himself *hisssss* like a snake. His fingers are in his ears because I don't think he likes the sound he's making and then the two of them push out through the door and Mum holds his reins as he gallops.

I put back the high-tops with blue laces.

Finished finished finished.

3 18 15 19 48

MUM IS VERY cross with the shoe lady but she doesn't say that to me. I am very cross with the shoe lady because she talked to Max when he was tightrope balancing and she pushed him off and down down down. *We'll try again* Mum says. *We'll try again another day.* I know that she means Dad will go and get everything and Max will stay at home and spin himself around and around until he's too dizzy to do that and then he'll watch something else spin around.

Mum takes out the sticky shoe-store Velcro-y picture from Max's special book and she puts it away in a plastic folder that's fat with pictures he does and doesn't like and then she gives him his special toy bug that buzzes gently when you touch its nose.

Max has lots and lots of special things.

He has

his special book with plastic pages and laminated sticky Velcro pictures to show him what's now and next

his special plastic pictures that Angelique is teaching him to exchange for things he wants

his special box full of things that light up and spin and glow like

his special squashy balls and glitter tubes and buzzy bugs to help him be a calm boy.

I have

my soccer trophies
my bright red bike with 21 gears
my books on detectives and codes and space
a lock on my bedroom door.

When Dad gets home from work he goes on his own and gets the shoes. I stay at home in my room because he wants to be *quick about it* and Max stays at home and spins. Mum pushes her fingers into her temples like she always does when her head is bursting.

Max gets the same shoes as always and forever and mine are black sneakers with black laces that give my fingers rope burn and I wish they were different.

7   12   21   5

THERE ARE TWENTY-ONE DAYS before school starts. Max hasn't been to school before. When Max was three he went to a nursery school but he melted and melted and melted day after day after day. His face was always puffy from crying and from hitting himself until the skin around his eyes was painted with blue bruises. Then Max bit another child and the nursery school asked Mum to come and pick him up. She cried afterward and Granny M came around and was calm and put the kettle on.

Granny M is Mum's mum and sometimes I think it's funny that Mum still has her mum who comes around and makes her tea. Granny M is like a little bird with twiggy arms in soft sweaters and legs draped in gray pants but she's like steel underneath, like when people stare at Max or when I haven't done my homework. Mum told her what had happened at the nursery school and I listened even though I was pretending to be working on codes in my notebook. Ahmed and Jamie and I had a whole new alphabet made of spiky symbols and dots and lines and I was trying to push all of the new letters into my head so I could write them secret notes in class. I put my face very close to the paper so I wasn't really looking at Mum and Granny M but I could hear everything they were saying.

Mum was hiccup-crying in little bursts and she said that Kelsey from the nursery school wanted extra training before she could be Max's helper again. Mum kept saying he's never bitten another child before, not even Frank. And I thought about the little pink and purple thumbprints on my arms from when Max is too excited or too hot or too cross and I didn't really think it mattered about the not-biting. Mum was trying to swallow tea but she couldn't make it go down right and Granny M gave her a thump on the back and Mum cried again and said she was too upset to even swallow a sip of tea and if you can't have a cup of tea in a crisis then what's the point of being British. And then she did a laugh that still sounded like a sob.

Then we saw doctors about Max and he didn't go back to that nursery school and he and Mum were stuck together like glue.

18   1   13   19   8   30   3   11   12   5

THERE ARE TWENTY DAYS before Max starts school and I am in my room listening to him shout and whirl and melt. The sound is bouncing and echoing up through the floorboards so I climb up and up the winding attic stairs until I can't hear his howls. The stairs creak and whine because we live in a ramshackle house. That's what Dad calls it and he rolls the r around in his mouth and lets it fly out with a flick of his tongue. Max laughs when Dad says it so he says it a lot. *My wife and my boys in our ramshackle house.* Dad made it sound beautiful, so when I looked up ramshackle on Google and it said *in a state of severe disrepair* I thought I must have found the wrong word.

The house has got strange crumbly bits and the walls lean in toward us and the floorboards groan when Max spins. The top room all the way up the attic stairs has a musty damp smell when it rains but no one but me goes up there now anyway so it doesn't matter. The front door is bright red because Mum and Dad let me choose when I was five and I loved red, and all the leaning-in walls are covered in framed pictures that I did at nursery school and some pencil scribbles by Max when he was a toddler that Dad says are definitely modern art. There are paintings that Mum did too, before she had us and lost the time she used to have all to herself.

She was an artist before she had Max and this damp-smelling room was her studio because she said the light from the slanted windows in the roof was perfect. She painted the universe. Stars and skies and great galaxies that change and shift every time you look at them until sometimes they look like something very far away and sometimes they look like something you've known all your life.

She used to have exhibitions in galleries and people would pay lots of money for her paintings and every time she sold one Dad would open a bottle of champagne and they would dance around the kitchen and drink from tall thin glasses. Once, she dipped her finger into the glass and put it into my mouth so I could taste it and it popped and burned and they both laughed when I stuck my tongue out and cried that I didn't like it. Then Mum put her arms around me and lifted me high up toward the ceiling and the three of us danced in a circle on the cold kitchen tiles.

When I was small, even smaller than Max, Mum still climbed these stairs in the morning while I played spaceships with Granny M or Dad or the nanny whose name I can't remember. Mum started the day in a clean blue shirt, always a soft blue shirt, and every time she came back down the stairs there were all the colors of a new painting decorating her clothes and her skin. The paint smelled sharp and sweet and even after she'd taken off her painting clothes it clung to her skin and hair.

Dad always wore a suit made from something scratchy and dark, with a shirt that stayed clean all day and sometimes a tie with pointed ends like a snake's tongue that he could flick into an impossible knot.

Before Max, he'd always be home to tuck me into bed and he would read me stories about an adventuring astronaut floating through the Milky Way in a crow-black sky, and about the boy detective Tintin who solved puzzles and codes to solve crimes. I loved them because all the clues fit together at the end and then everything was okay. Dad told me when I was old enough he'd teach me a special type of code for computers because that's what he does all day at work but I'm old enough now and I'm still waiting.

Then Mum's blue shirt started stretching out farther and farther away from her as her belly grew a new person and Mum stopped going upstairs quite as much. Instead she would help me paint paper planets to hang from my ceiling and together we mapped out the stars on my walls. When Max was born she stopped going upstairs and she didn't sell any more paintings. Dad started wearing his suit so much it was like it had become stitched to his skin and there were no more bedtime stories because Dad wouldn't be back from work in time and Mum would be with Max.

And now I sit on the floor in Mum's studio surrounded by dried-out tubes of paint that have lost their smell and paintings that she never sold and I scribble my codes onto a huge blank snowy-white canvas. My favorite code is the number-letters-spiral cipher which is just about the easiest code in the universe but it's my favorite anyway. Cipher is just another word for code really but I love the way it sounds. I don't know what the hardest code in the universe is but I want to be the one to invent it. I don't want anyone to be able to crack it, and I'll use it to write everything that burns inside me on days like this.

6 9 7 8 20

THERE ARE NINETEEN DAYS before Max starts school. Dad has just got home from work and he promised he'd be in time for dinner but dinner is *finished*. Mum and Dad are having a whispery-hissed fight about Max and about *what is best*. Their fight is the loudest since Max gave Mum a black eye without meaning to hit but still hitting, watery swelling puffing along her cheek and inkblue teardrop bruises spilling in a starry galaxy around her temple.

I peep through the banister while Max sits in his room and peacefully rolls a marble around and around a plastic peanut butter jar lid. Dad stands stiff like a soldier but his hands are stuffed deep in his pockets so that the stitches make little crackles. Mum throws her arms wide like she's about to give him a hug so big it would wrap around and around him but instead she just starts to cry. She howls that all she wants is to take us away somewhere beautiful. Dad makes these odd little chirrupy shushing noises that sound more like a bird than a man but Mum doesn't notice the birdman standing in her living room. *You need to help me.* She says it over and over. Her eyes are swimmy and full and she gulps air like she's drowning.

I don't want to watch anymore but I can't move without them noticing me so I sit so still that muscles start to scream. Mum wipes her eyes and sniffs and says *it'll be okay won't it? I just wish we could get away from all of this.* And in that moment I wish my piggy bank that's shaped like a soccer ball had more money in it so I could take her on a trip far away from our ramshackle house.

8   5   12   16

THERE ARE EIGHTEEN DAYS before Max starts school. Dad tells me that he's going to start doing more for me and Max and won't that be nice, more time together. *Mum's been feeling tired, champ, so we have to help out more than we do right now.* He looks a bit guilty when he says this and he starts tugging at his tie so that the knot gets tighter and tighter.

He tries to put me and Max to bed while Mum watches TV and it all goes wrong. Max's bath isn't right and it never is but Dad doesn't sing the bath song or splash the water with a pat of his hand to show that it's really okay. He doesn't put on the bedtime light show that speckles the stars across Max's ceiling and bathes his little face in all of the universe. Everything falls out of place and I sit on my bed listening to the screams that echo from room to room until I hear Mum's soft voice sing a lullaby that rises up over Max's sounds and hushes them back into his mouth.

I brush my teeth and put on my pajamas and read four pages of my book and have my half hour on the iPad which has a cracked screen from when Max flew it down the stairs *whoosh bang*. I time myself and no one comes to tell me the time's up so I have forty-five minutes instead and then I turn out my light because no one comes to tell me to do that either.

I hear Dad slip out from Max's room and his socks padding on the floorboards outside my room. I pretend to be asleep as he puts his face around my door. I squint through half-closed lashes and through the blur I can see his tears.

20   18   5   1   19   21   47   34

THERE ARE SEVENTEEN DAYS before Max starts school and Mum and I are going to a flea market to hunt for treasure. Mum wakes me up early, even earlier than for school, and the sun is painting the sky with orange streaks. Dad has taken the day off and we leave him and Max at the kitchen table eating breakfast and walk to the train station just the two of us with no Max strapped into his too-big stroller or flapping and bouncing as he walks next to me and taking up all my space. It's just me and Mum and she holds my hand even though I'm ten.

At the station she buys me a hot chocolate with extra whipped cream that is piled up like a cloud in the cup and on the platform she talks to me about my favorite things. We talk about space and the universe and how it would take 800 years to fly to Pluto in a normal plane and how the sunset on Mars is blue. We don't have to sing songs or talk with our hands or hold Max's stiff-melting body when the rumble of the train on the tracks makes him scream. When we get on the train she taps our secret code onto the palm of my hand and I tap it back.

Our code is Morse code and it was invented hundreds of years ago before telephones and texts and emails but the people who used it then had machines that tapped out messages made of short taps and long taps that they listened to. It was for sending messages to places far away, and you can even do it with flashlights by making long flashes and short flashes but Mum and I use it when we're right next to each other so it's special and it's ours. We use our hands and Mum taught it to me when I was little and we were learning to speak to Max with our hands. We all had to learn how to say things like *finished* and *thank you* and *cookie*. But when I was scared or angry or crying or lonely, Mum could take my hand in hers and the taps and

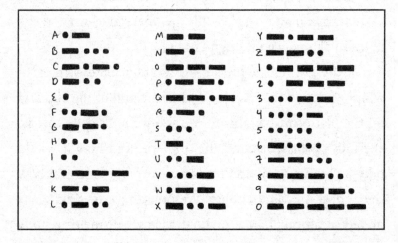

Morse code

lines *dot-dot dot-dash-dot-dot dash-dot-dash-dash* meant she loved me. Just between us.

When we get to the flea market we walk through a world of colors and shapes and noises and we don't have to make it all go away, because Max isn't with us. It feels like the world has been switched on. I can smell dust and age and when a man drops a chair we don't have to leave because of the bang. Mum finds me a whole set of Superman comics from forever ago and their pages are yellowed with all the years since they were printed but there isn't a single crease lining the paper. I imagine the child who had them all those years ago being so careful with the delicate sheets that felt like flower petals and I hold them in my hands like they are made of glass.

Mum can spot a bargain at a thousand paces and as she wanders through the tightly packed aisles of people burrowing through piles of clothes and knickknacks and ornaments she's the first to spot a glint of color peeking up from the bottom of a cardboard box. She puts her hand in and gently digs down until she frees her prize. She holds a little scrap of light, a luminous orb filled with arches and swirls and bubbles. Mum says it's a paperweight but it looks like it's a piece of magic to me. It flings out its colors like a magician pulling handkerchief after handkerchief from his sleeves just like the one at Jamie's eighth birthday party. I'd wanted a magician for my party but in the end we went to the movies and Dad had to stay at home with Max.

When we get home Mum puts the paperweight on a shelf in my room next to my soccer trophies and its light bounces off my star-print walls where the constellations swirl and twinkle. My room is somewhere Max can't go and it's full of my treasures. I have a padlock on the outside of the door to keep it locked when I'm out and he's not, and the padlock has a code to open it. It's 0223 because that's my birthday and Max doesn't know that.

Now my room is even better than before. Mum stands back and declares the paperweight *looks just right* and it's like it had been made especially for our house and for my room. It slots right into its place like a piece of a jigsaw puzzle and I glow inside because it's like magic and Mum bought it just for me and it looks *just right*.

19 15 18 47 25

IT IS FIFTEEN DAYS before Max starts school and the sun is peering pathetically from behind fat clouds. Ahmed and Jamie are still on vacation and it feels like they've been away forever and I'm the only one from our gang left. I am bored in the house so we have to go out so I can be bored outside instead because Mum says being indoors is making me loopy and loud. I go and see what Dad's doing but he's working on his computer even though it's the weekend and he doesn't want to show me what he's doing or talk to me about how everyone on Earth would weigh two and a half times as much if they were on Jupiter or that space is completely silent.

I want to go on my own but Mum says *we should all go out together* and *it'll be lovely* and *it's such a beautiful day isn't it*. It's definitely not but I wait while she shows Max the park card and then the swing card because he likes that one the most. He flies up higher on the swings than even I can because Max isn't scared about falling off. When Max swings he makes his noises which I know sound funny like a baby and an animal all jumbled together with a laugh in his mouth and sometimes he lets go but he never falls.

We can walk to the park because it's just at the end of our street except Max doesn't walk there. He goes in his too-big stroller so he can't run off and away to find blue cars and red buses. I hate the stroller because it doesn't look right and people stare at it and then again and then they go *oh*. I have my soccer ball so I kick it boom out of the door and I pelt into the summer-hot-damp morning street because no one will stop me. I run past Mr. Next Door who is actually named Mark who studied art at college with Mum and now they live right next to each other and *isn't life full of coincidences?* When we moved here Mum said she saw Mark and they each they did a little double-take jump that meant *I know you!*

Mark's walking his supercool hairy dog who is named Neil. Mark comes around most weeks and he and Mum talk about different types of paint and drink tea and I get to play with Neil and he's the smartest dog in the whole wide universe. I think Neil is a strange name for a dog but I'd love a dog like him to pitter-patter after me as I zoom on my bike and nose a ball like a doggy soccer player so I'd always have someone to shoot goals against. Mum says we have enough on our plates without having a dog too so I can't have my very own Neil. Max likes Neil which is weird because dogs make noises and jump about suddenly and Max hates it when people do that.

I reach the park and I sprint past the playground to the

grassy field that is my soccer stadium. I dribble and shoot and volley and I am Messi and the crowd around me roars as I score goal after goal until Mum is there and she says *Max wanted to walk with you* and I say *Max wants the swings* and then I run away again to win the World Cup. There are bigger boys without their shirts on playing soccer near me. They have shaved the sides of their heads so just a stripe of tufty hair grows on top and I wonder if Mum will let me do that too. I want them to notice my magic feet and tell me I'm the best ten-year-old they've ever seen play soccer and can they play with me so I can teach them how to be as good.

Max goes on his swings and he makes his noises as he flies. The boys are sweating and they stop their game and they don't look at me even though I'm scoring the winning goal against Brazil but they look at Max making his happy swing noises. They use bad words when they talk but then they use the worst word of all about Max which begins with an R and Mum said I could never ever say. Then they laugh and laugh and laugh. And I laugh too. They look at me and I laugh with them and they grin and say *all right* and I play soccer with them and I score while Max swings and doesn't care at all.

After our game the boys give me high fives and then they lollop off with their shirts around their shoulders.

I walk home with Max and I let him hold my soccer ball but he wants to hold my hand so we do that too and I want to whisper *I'm sorry* but I don't.

13 15 14 11 5 25 2 44 54

IT IS FOURTEEN DAYS before Max starts school. I am going to be a Year Six at Wolverton Juniors. *You are top of the ladder* Dad says. *The monkeys on the highest branch of the tree.*

Max isn't coming to Wolverton Juniors with me. Mum and Dad talked about all the different places he could go to school and that they could send him to a boarding school far far away where he'd have a different bedroom and someone else would coax him into the bath and read his favorite stories and sing him songs while he fell asleep. Mum said *no way* so they went to see another school near us. They left me and Max with Granny M which was okay but Max thought it was strange because he bounced about looking for Mum and flapping a straw in his hand like he does when he knows something isn't the same and he isn't sure about it at all. Granny M's come around quite a lot this summer and she says Mum needs some time to herself. Mum never used to leave Max but now sometimes she slips out of the door superquiet like a mouse and when she comes back she never says where she's been but she's just as tired as if she'd taken Max with her anyway.

Mum and Dad got back from seeing Max's new school and were very excited and told me and Max about a soft playroom and that there was a bubbly swimming pool. I thought that was a stupid thing to tell Max because he hates having a bath but he didn't seem to mind. Mum said *Maxy they have your special toys there and all the teachers can talk with their hands and there's a room of lights that change color when you press a button!* He put his head to one side and they showed him a new special book called *This Is My School* which has pictures of the new school and some of the students and all of his teachers.

There are more teachers at Max's new school than at mine but there aren't as many children. Dad says *they're not all teachers, some of them are for helping children with other things like running or talking.* Max can only do one of those but he's very good at it. I said *he wouldn't need help with that* and Dad laughed and then said that he thought *maybe the talking not-teacher will mean Max could learn to say things to us* and I thought that would be better than humming and wailing and making the noises he made on the swings.

I wasn't sure if the new school would make Max suddenly start using his words with his hands and his mouth because ever since Max stopped going to nursery school

Angelique has come to see Max twice a week and he can't even say c-a-t cat. Angelique is a *speech and language therapist* which sounds scary but she isn't. Angelique comes on Tuesdays and Thursdays and always Tuesdays and Thursdays except when she goes to visit her family in France but she doesn't do that often.

When she first came to our house she came in and sat on the floor right next to Max and just handed him a light-up windmill. My muscles turned to stone and my stomach went swoop because she was sitting there in his air and he needs his space especially from new people unless he's decided he wants to sit on top of you all of a sudden. But Max turned his face to her and took the windmill and it lit up in his hand and he giggled and Angelique said *we're going to be friends, aren't we Max?* and Max put his tongue on the windmill as if he was checking the taste of its colors. Now he waits at the window for her to come twice a week every week and she says he's on the very edge of doing something amazing.

10   15   25

IT'S THIRTEEN DAYS before Max starts school. Today is Tuesday and Angelique's sitting in the kitchen and Max is sitting too. Max is supposed to give her a plastic card with a picture of a toy he wants, but he won't do that yet. It's a swap, a card for a toy. If Angelique puts her hand over his and helps him to pass her a card then he does it but that's just copying. Angelique says she has to break things down for Max and then he'll be able build it up himself soon. *Break down a task into tiny pieces, Frank. Then he'll learn to put the pieces together again and do it all for himself.*

I know Max is desperate for a ball that has a swirl of glitter swimming in its belly. Angelique has two cards and all Max has to do is pick one up, even if it's just the one with a picture of a paper clip on it and not the one with a shiny ball. One day he'll be able to pick up the right plastic card and hand it over and then one day after that he'll be able to pick up a card that says *I want* and then add the right card next to it on a plastic strip that he hands over. And then after that he's meant to be able to make all sorts of sentences and hand them to us, but Max won't even do this stupid first part. He keeps reaching and reaching straight for the ball and I think he might melt right then and there on the kitchen floor and I'm annoyed because I want to get some orange juice. But Angelique puts her hand over his again and guides it down and his little fingers scrabble at the plastic card and pass it to her and Angelique grins and she says and signs *ball* when she gives his glitter ball in return. Max is alight with joy.

Angelique turns to me and tells me that things I find easy like getting dressed or asking for what I want are harder for Max, and I think in my head *I know that* but I nod and say outside my head that he needs things *broken down*. Angelique smiles and nods when I say that and says I'm a good brother and I don't tell her about the soccer boys in the park because I get hot liquidy sparks shooting inside when I think about doing things like that but I do them anyway.

19 20 1 18 48

IT IS ELEVEN DAYS before Max starts school. Mum tells Max that he's going to wear a T-shirt with the name of his school on it and she shows Max the T-shirt but he won't touch it. She puts it in his drawer on top of his other clothes and says *it's a nice uniform*. I look at it and it has stars on it where my uniform has letters. I tell Max his uniform is cool and Mum and Dad smile but Max just wants to put the washing machine on. Anyway there's no way Max will wear his school T-shirt because he thinks he only wears one T-shirt. It is gray with yellow stripes and he has fifteen of them because I counted.

Mum picks up Max's school T-shirt again and she counts the stars with him but he doesn't care. She tells him he will only go to school for the mornings and she shows him morning with her hands and then she says he'll go for the whole day when he's ready. She shows him his clock with the sun and moon and stars and moves the pointy hands with his hands and says it all again. She says the name of his school very s l o w l y and then very quickly and she shows him his school book. Max only likes one book really and it's *Goodnight Moon* and I hate it because it's for babies and Max is five.

One day last year Mum pushed Max in his too-big stroller to pick me up from school instead of me walking home with Jamie and Ahmed. When Max saw me he held his baby book up high toward me and squealed. Noah laughed and said *is that your brother?* even though he knew it was. And I shouted **NO** and I ran all the way home and far away from Max. I was angry with Noah because Max was proud of coming to pick me up but I was angrier with Max for being proud and angriest with Mum for bringing Max to school.

When Max is watching the washing whirling around and around I go and look at his new book that tells him all about his new school so he's not surprised when he gets there. The school looks different and more fun than Wolverton Juniors. The picture of it from the outside shows a low white building with round windows and it looks just like a spaceship. The inside is spaceship-y too with rainbow lights and shiny sleek touchscreens in the white-walled classrooms. The book is written like Max is saying it. *I can use the Jacuzzi. I learn on the iPad. I can ask for snacks.*

There's a picture of a boy that's not Max and he's handing over a picture of a cookie and he's getting a cookie from a teacher but that won't work because Max doesn't like those cookies. Max won't like that picture because it's not him and those aren't his cookies. Max's cookies live in a red tin with yellow dots and Angelique is teaching Max to ask for them with a plastic card. Max will have to take his tin into school because once Granny M put Max's cookies in a different tin and he wouldn't eat them because it wasn't right and then he melted. I wanted to tell Mum and Dad about the tin but they were talking with their heads down low and Mum had taken out Max's new school T-shirt and was smoothing it with her hands over and over.

6 21 18 25

IT IS SEVEN DAYS before school starts. Mum is reading
a story with Max curled up on the floor in the living room
and then she shows him new things for school and does
Angelique's homework with him. It takes hours. She has
to print some new Max cards and she makes important
Max phone calls where her voice goes low. She and Max
are glued together and it makes my brain go red. Max's
squashy balls and spinning wheels and light-up sparkly
sticks are everywhere and even though they throw glitter
shadows on the carpet I still manage to trip and fall a hundred times.

When I hit the rug for the hundred and first time I
throw a whirly little plastic spinner at the wall and it cracks
and smashes and its silver water streaks down to the floor
and Max howls and starts to hit his head like he does when
he's melting into fury or when he hears something that
seems to make his brain burn. Mum gets out his favorite
thing ever which is thick paper he can't rip and wax cray-
ons which smear their colors on the paper. He gasps and

32

he sits and draws things that look like things we know and *he's just so clever like that isn't he?* says Mum. *Sit down and draw with us* she says and her hands make quick practiced perfect pencil strokes across her paper until there's a Lego man jumping onto the back of a tiger.

I want to see a movie and go bowling and swimming and not stay in the howling jungle with this wildboy everywhere I turn. I ask and ask and ask and I sing it and shout it and squeak it and shriek it and Mum says *not today not today not today*. Then she snaps and she uses a voice that isn't low but it's very quick and she shouts

Frank don't you ever think about anything

how could we do those things with Max?

the dark of the movie theater

and

the flicker of the screen

and

the noise of the movie

and

the clunk of the pins

and

the flash of the lights

and

the splash of the water

and

he hates baths you know that

and

will you just stop and think just think about what you're asking and

go read a book or

play on that stupid iPad or

watch TV or

shoot goals at the garden fence but will you just

STOP.

So I **STOP** and I go into the kitchen. I find a red pen and I draw hieroglyphics and pictures like the cavemen did and I write my name and I try to write how unfair everything is but I can't make the words click together into sense so I write all the words that are bad and cruel and nasty and I scrawl and scribble and I roar and howl and shriek and fight but not with my voice and I use the pen until every inch of wall that I can reach is a sketch of the raging hot screams inside me and the ink is fading pale from the nib.

Mum goes to make tea and sees what I've done. I hear the sound of a hurled teacup shattering against the wall and I hide in my room with my comforter over my head so my bed is a cozy tent but my heart is thumping in my ears. The stairs creak and thud and there's a shuffle of feet outside my door but it doesn't swing open and bounce off my dresser like it did when Dad came into my room after I'd poured my chocolate and banana milkshake over the sofa when I was five and they'd brought Max home forever. Mum taps our Morse code onto the door so I know it's her and then pushes it open like nothing's wrong but it's very wrong because she's crying and she says *oh Frank I'm so sorry my boy I'm so sorry* and she sits on my bed and she strokes my head even though it's covered in my soccer comforter and she whispers over and over that she's sorry and I start to curl into her words.

13 1 7 9 3

THE NEXT DAY Dad takes a day off from work again. We go on a train and leave Mum and Max behind with their books and their stories and his shouting. I feel a funny tug when I look at Mum's tired face and the kitchen walls all scrawled with my fury and I think I don't deserve to go on a train to Brighton to see the sea but Dad gives me a smile that squeezes that feeling out of me.

At the beach I eat fish and chips from newspaper and they taste like the salted air. Dad and I line up on the pier to go on rides that make my stomach swoop and I can feel the chips swirling in my stomach. We go on the tea-cups and I like spinning then, when I can see the world whirling around me and the faces of the crowds being whooshed into a blur. When my stomach is feeling a little bit less swoopy from the food and spinning we buy cotton candy and it melts into pink streaks in my mouth and it sticks in bright sticky sugar lumps to my teeth but it doesn't matter. Then Dad leans in and asks me with a wink if I'd like to have some more chips.

I toe the waves on the beach and the water licks me to shivers so I don't swim even though I had put my trunks on under my pants. Instead I watch gulls scribbling themselves over the sea and beaking their fish dinners. I copy their *caw caw* call and throw them the last of my vinegary chips and they fight each other for the scraps in an air-beating flap of feathered wings. I do the *caw caw* again and Dad laughs and tries to do it too but he sounds more like our old cat that yowled around the house asking for food. We walk back along the beachfront and see performers with painted metal faces and robot hands and magic tricks that make Dad give a low whistle *wow*. The pier is a whirl of colors that spin out and dance into new shapes in the splashes of sea between the boards under my feet and that's real magic.

When we get home Max is already in bed and Mum and next-door Mark are having a drink in the living room. Mark has brought Neil, and I stroke his gray tangled-fur head and I can't stop talking about the performers and the seagulls and I accidentally tell them that I had vinegary chips twice but no one seems to mind at all.

23 9 12 4

THERE ARE THREE DAYS before school starts. Things are better because Ahmed and Jamie are back from their vacations and we're at Jamie's house. Jamie went to Spain. Ahmed went to Bangladesh. He shows me some pictures on his phone and says *man it was hot and I didn't even have to wear shoes*. I thought Max would like that and probably Mum would like it too because then she wouldn't have to see shoe store lady again.

Ahmed said he'd actually been kind of bored in Bangladesh because he was with his boring grandparents and aunts and uncles and they sat around in the heat all day and talked and laughed because they don't see each other very much but Ahmed didn't have anything to do except be hot and not wear shoes. Jamie said he'd wrestled a shark in Spain and Ahmed and I just laughed at that. Last year Jamie went to Florida and wrestled an alligator but his brother said *in your dreams* when he heard so we don't believe Jamie much anymore. Jamie's brother is fifteen and he shaves the sides of his head but not the top and has high-tops with long laces. Ahmed has five brothers and sisters and he's the baby even though he's ten. Neither of them has a Max. I'm the only one with him.

We are all together again but we don't know what to do with ourselves because there's a whole summer between us and it's raining. We watch new videos on YouTube with the volume up and no one says *Jamie turn it down* and we play Minecraft and use blocks to build a new world with endless towers and it's better than when it's just me but we are loopy from being indoors.

When the rain stops we go for a bike ride in the Wilderness. It's not really the wilderness, but it's like it. The grass is all scrubby and rabbits kick and jump with velvet legs and the trees are wild and spring out from the turns of the path like in a pop-up book. Ahmed says the trees are thousands of years old and I believe him. Some parts of the Wilderness are bumpy and hilly and some are bare and open and others are dark and tangled and I like those the best. Once we tried to build a den in the tangles but we didn't really know how and all we had was a sheet that Jamie stole from his mum, and some sticks that were too small. So now we just swoosh on our bikes and don't stop until our hearts go *beatbeatbeat* too fast and I have to shout *stop!* with the last of my air.

When we are airless we sit in the damp scrub which smells like the rain and hot leaves and a steaming kettle and a bit like Mr. Next Door's dog Neil. Today Jamie wants to make a fire and maybe we can trap a rabbit and cook it and eat it with our teeth and fingers tearing the meat and the juices dribbling down our chins. We are wildboys surviving in the wild woods. When I don't come home and Dad comes to find me he'll see me living in a den wearing rabbit skins and a necklace of bones and my face streaked with rabbit blood and he'll go home and tell Mum that Frank is a true wildboy and he's not coming back to walls and doors and bedtime and special books and melting. Mum will be sad and she will go and buy me high-tops and a PlayStation and she'll cry real tears but I still won't go home.

Jamie has a red plastic lighter he stole from his brother. He makes a nest of leaves and twigs and we wait for them to hiss into sparks but the lighter won't click and throw out its flame. We don't feel so wild anymore because everyone knows you need fire to live in the wilderness and cook rabbits. Jamie clicks the lighter again and shakes it and then chucks it at Ahmed and says *it must be a dud*. Ahmed shakes it and clicks it and a little blue flame flicks its tongue from the silver tip. Jamie doesn't like that and he shouts at Ahmed and Ahmed shouts back and I put my fingers in my ears because I wanted us to be wildboys of the woods together, even just for today.

Then Jamie throws a shower of wet leaves at Ahmed and Ahmed throws a handful of dirt back at him and no one is cross anymore. We throw great chunks of the forest floor at each other until we're panting and covered with mud and bits of trees. Ahmed and Jamie look like wild-boys and I know I must too. I smear mud on my face and let out a Tarzan shout that bounces off the trees and fills the damp air around us. Ahmed and Jamie copy, and then Ahmed does a wolf howl that sounds almost real. We shout and whoop and howl and charge at each other like bulls until I feel lighter than I have all summer.

Ahmed tells me and Jamie to go and get the driest twigs and leaves we can find, and by the time we get back he's made a circle of stones for us to put them in. He builds the sticks up so they look like a little triangular house. He says he saw how to do it on TV and then he takes Jamie's brother's red lighter and Jamie doesn't say anything this time. We all watch with eyes like saucers and faces swiped with muddy streaks as Ahmed coaxes the flames like they're an animal. They're reluctant and timid at first but Ahmed blows gently on the little licks of fire and they start to roar.

We warm our hands by our very own fire and keep feeding it the dry twigs. It eats them hungrily until we haven't got anything more to give it and it spits and stutters until it's nothing but glowing embers and Ahmed stamps them down with his thick boots until the faint orange fades to gray. Then I take a stick and I scratch 23 9 12 4 into the earth and Jamie and Ahmed and I sign our initials. 10 and 1 and 6.

14 15 20 29 6 1 9 18

I TAKE MY bike and pedal it home so very slowly away from the wildboy Wilderness. I can see the lights in the kitchen bright and steady through the window and I want a spitting hot flame flicker fire to light me instead. It is time for dinner and Mum and Dad and Max are sitting around the table in the glow of the evening sun and I am on the outside looking in.

I slink into the house like a stealth ninja because I don't want to sit in the kitchen and eat with Max and see him taste his food first with his nose so the smell doesn't surprise him in his mouth. Max doesn't use a knife and fork or even a spoon because he won't hold the metal or plastic or rubber without saying no no no but not with words. He eats with his hands in the same way that I am not allowed to and in the same way that wildboy Frank would eat his fat-dripping meaty rabbit by the Wilderness fire. But I am not a wildboy and I am not a slinking stealth ninja because Mum straightaway says *hello Frank good job for being home on time* and she's calling me into the kitchen so I skulk in like a hunter stalking prey but she says *is there something wrong with your shoulder?* so I stop and glower and sit down at the table and leave wildboy hunter ninja Frank for another day.

Max has his special plate and I have any plate because I don't mind. Max's plate has Mickey Mouse on it but Mickey's face is all bubbled because Dad put a hot pan on top of it by mistake and Max didn't ever want a different plate even when Dad went and bought the exact same one. Max knew it wasn't right and I didn't know how he could know that. Max likes four foods and they're not healthy and they won't make him grow up big and strong. I once told him that he needed to grow his muscles like Popeye and eat spinach but then I thought about Max with muscles and I didn't say anything else about spinach ever again.

Max likes to eat one kind of potato chip called Quavers, mashed potatoes, plain cookies and French fries with no red sauce. *A good spread of potato there* says Dad when he puts Max's plate of French fries and potato chips in front of him. *Sampling the varieties. Next year we could throw in a baked potato, eh?* Then Dad puts peas on the table too but Max never eats his greens because he won't eat any colors. I still have to eat vegetables and I don't think that's fair but life's not fair says Dad and I think that's true or Max wouldn't be here.

20   15   44   29   2   18   9   7   8   49

IT IS THE night before Max starts school. After dinner Mum puts out Max's starry school T-shirt and my Wolverton Juniors sweater and polo shirt. Tomorrow I will take my bike to be a Year Six top-of-the-tree monkey and Max will go in a bus that comes right to the door and takes him away to the spaceship school with the room of lights and the iPads and the little bubbly swimming pool.

In Max's special school book it says that a lady named Rhoda will help him on the bus and there is a picture of Rhoda and she is old and smiling and wears a bright yellow vest over her sweater and it's like the kind the builders next door wore last year. Max hated those vests because they were loud and zingy yellow. Rhoda's vest is too bright and it will hurt Max's eyes and he will have to squeeze them shut so he won't see Rhoda or be able to look out of the window on the drive to school and Max loves to look out of the window and make his noises when he sees blue cars or red buses because they're the best ones.

I tell Mum that Max won't be able to look at Rhoda and

doesn't she remember next door's builders and she does a deep sigh from somewhere sad but nothing else happens. Later she brings me a hot chocolate and lets me drink it in bed but her eyes are far away and I can't find the words to tell her that I understand, just a little bit. So I use our special code and I tap out three letters on her palm and she tells me she loves me too.

6 1 12 41 9 14 7

IN THE MORNING it is school and I put on my polo shirt with its letters and my red Wolverton sweater which is new because it says Year Six on the back so all the little children know who is at the top of the tree. I wolf down my cereal and my breakfast banana which I have every morning before school. There are new cards in Max's special book and they are *bus* and *school*. Max isn't wearing his starry school T-shirt and his hand is red and bitten so I know Mum has tried. I heard him screaming this morning while I was in the bathroom brushing my teeth and washing my face and I splashed the water in the sink so the droplets flew up and speckled the mirror and I watched the tiny rippling waves in the sink instead of listening to the shrieks.

Max is wearing his new shoes that look the same as his old shoes so he doesn't know about the new part and they light up blue in a flash like he likes. I think it's weird that he doesn't notice new shoes but he notices a new plate but no one can ever explain Max to me. He eats his breakfast Quavers and drops plain cookies on the floor and draws a cat with green eyes and ginger fur just like our old cat Pernikitty that died when he was three and how does he remember? He looks at the cards in his book and I know he's looking but he doesn't turn his head and look straight at them and instead he looks at them from the side of his eyes and he flaps and rocks and he's worried about everything being new new new. I tell him *new school* and I tell him it will be fun. I talk to him about the room of cool lights and the iPads. Max doesn't want to listen to me and he pushes my words away with his hands and I give up. He's a scaredy boy today.

I can't find my pencil case anywhere at all. I know I left it on the side table in the kitchen and I want to find it now so I can cycle fast with Jamie and Ahmed so we can play soccer in the playground before the bell rings. I ask Mum in a quiet voice and then I say it louder and louder until I'm almost shouting but she's not listening because she's fussing and getting all the things she thinks Max needs and Max is trying to show her his picture of his cat. I'm getting more anxious by the minute because I can't turn up on my first day in Year Six without the right things.

A minibus pulls up outside but it's not red so Max won't like it. There aren't as many seats as the bus I went on for the Year Five trip to the Science Museum where everything was something and you could touch anything without being in trouble and I thought that Max would like it here except for all the noise. I got him an ammonite from the museum store, an arching swirl of frozen history, and Max loves to run his thumb along its ridges.

I can see through the window that there are other children on the bus already and some of them are all wrapped up in strange seat belts that look like the tangled trees from the Wilderness. Some of them have their fingers jammed into their ears and some of them are stabbing at iPads without looking up at all even though the bus has stopped and the driver has put the hazard lights on so that the orange flashes through the window and bounces around the kitchen. Mum says they're early but I know they're not actually because I can see the big orange kitchen clock.

Mum still isn't listening to me and I still haven't found my pencil case. So I clamber and stand on a chair to stretch up tall to shout out loud so she'll see me and hear me for just that one moment. But Mum doesn't look up at me so I wave my arms in the air. The chair has a leg that sways and wobbles side to side so it's not for standing on but I am Frank the monkeyboy who can climb to the top of the highest monkey puzzle tree and I am Frank the wildboy who wears rabbit skins and swings from vines shouting out a wildboy cry and I am Frank the spaceboy who jumps from asteroid to asteroid at zero gravity. Then Mum sees me and she gasps *Frank* and I am Frank ordinaryboy and then I turn and then I tumble. And then there are cookies everywhere and I land on them and they go crunch and my arm goes crunchcrack and Mum goes *Christ*.

2 12 15 44 4

MUM CALLS FOR Dad in a voice I don't know and he runs in with shaving foam icing his face and his tie isn't a tie because it's not tied. The doorbell is going **trring trring trring** and I am on the floor with my arm full of stinging bees and the cookies scattered and the chair upside down and suddenly but not really suddenly my head is all syrupy wet with blood. Max is starting to flap his hands like a broken bird and the doorbell rings **trring trring trring** again and Dad goes *Christ*. Mum says *help Frank, do something* and then she runs to the door and a lady says *you're really supposed to bring him out, are you having some trouble?* and I think that must be Rhoda and I think that my arm looks like Sam's arm when he fell off the swing and it's all loose and alien.

I am thinking too much and not at all because everything has happened and nothing is happening. Mum is in the kitchen with the lady who is Rhoda from the picture and her vest is very yellow and Max covers his eyes and does a wail song. I want to say that it's too bright but my teeth are stuck together and I might be sick.

Dad is holding whimpering Max in his arms and he's saying *Frank Frank Frank* and I think he might have been saying it for a long time. Rhoda will think we're all bonkers and she is looking at me on the floor with my alien arm and all the cookies and splashy blood from my head and now Max is a howling animal and Dad is foamy and Mum is doing a hiccup-cry, but Rhoda says *oh dear* and she takes off her vest and turns it inside out and says *well I can make that better, shall we go to school now Max?* She says it with her hands and she says it with her mouth and she's kind and we all know that right then. And Max is wriggling down from Dad and taking one of her talking hands and he's trotting like a little horse with Rhoda.

Dad stops saying *Frank* and Mum stops hiccupping and my arm stops pinging and zapping but I still know it's there. Time isn't ticktocking at all, except for all around Max as he bouncy trots to the hall and out the front door and then the spell explodes and Mum rushes out with Max's backpack which has cars all over it in a hundred different colors but they're not too bright and he loves it.

And then Dad is scooping me up which makes me scream from deep down in my belly which is the first noise I've made since I crunched and crashed to the floor and he goes *oh god Frank I'm so sorry* and he puts me in the front seat of the car and when he leans over to do up my seat belt my arm gives a fresh scream of pain and shaving foam drips from Dad's face onto my pants. The blood from my head drips too and it blooms in the foam like a snowy battleground. Mum gets into the driver's seat and she grips the steering wheel so tightly that the bones are bursting white from her knuckles. Then all of a sudden we vroom in the car to the hospital faster than the speed of light.

2 18 15 11 5 14

MUM SAYS DAD has called work to say not today so he can stay at home in case Max has trouble at his new school and Mum calls Wolverton Juniors while she's helping me out of the car and she tells them what has happened. It sounds cool when I hear it all pieced together for the school receptionist. My arm is throbbing like my bones are made of hot metal but I don't mind so much because it's just me and Mum. I don't mind one little tiny bit that I am missing before-bell soccer with Jamie and Ahmed and probably Sam too.

When we get to the hospital we go to the waiting room but the lady behind the desk takes one look at my battle-ground pants and my bendy arm and my bloody head and we don't have to wait in that room. I've never been to a hospital before, not until today. When Max was born I didn't visit him because Mum didn't even stay in the hospital for a single night. Everything went so well, she beamed, that they let us home right away. Mum must come here with Max for some of his appointments because she knows where everything is and she even smiles at some of the staff but she looks at them the same way Max sometimes looks at people, without really looking. One of the smiling staff even says it's nice to see her.

Someone put my arm in a white sling that feels like bedsheets and it hurt when they did it but now feels better cradled in cotton. We are in a little cubicle with a curtain you can swoosh around to make a room and when it's closed people say *knock knock* rather than knocking because there isn't a door. The curtain is covered in lions and tigers and trees and a swoop of sky and little kids might think they were in a jungle but I just count the animals. I get to forty-seven before Mum says something and I don't hear but I lose track of the creature count. I think she's waiting for the phone to ring and the new school to say come and get this boy **NOW** but then Dad calls and tells us Max is safely at school and he is going to clean up all the cookies and the blood which is *everywhere* and I think I'd like to see because it's like a horror movie but in our house. Mum hangs up her phone and says there's an egg on my forehead and I touch it with my fingers and feel a hot lump of bruise and my hand is damp with a squashed berry smear.

The doctor comes and says *knock knock* and she looks at my head and says that she'll glue it up and I laugh and laugh because I think of her fixing me with a glue stick from her doctor's pencil case and Mum says *I think they need to look at your brain you silly thing* and that makes me laugh more and even the doctor says very seriously that I might have laughitis and that there might not be a cure and then she laughs and says she's caught it. My arm still pings and zaps in its sling but this is fun and I get to have an X-ray. I am excited about seeing my bones and I don't even mind when they have to cut off my new red Year Six sweater with scissors and I see my arm is a fat slug with my skin stretched on top.

Mum walks and I whizz down the hospital corridors to the X-ray room on a special bed with wheels pushed by a man named Mick who has a moustache and a tattoo of a lion on his arm. He asks me about school and soccer and movies and then he tells me about how when he used to go to the movies his mother would give him enough money to buy a ticket for one of the best seats at the back but he'd buy a cheaper seat and spend the rest on candy. All the candy had names that meant I could taste them as he talked, like pineapple cubes and aniseed twists and barley sugar and rosy apples and I forget about my buzzy arm and my egg head.

When we get to the X-ray room Mick gives me a wink and strolls away humming into the twistyturny white halls. I am not so excited about seeing my bones now because the lady who takes the picture wants me to move my arm and I can't taste the candy anymore so I remember that it hurts. I put my arm on a silver table and Mum has to wear a funny apron to stop the X-rays from zapping her inside but it's not funny enough to stop my arm from screaming and the noise comes from my mouth when the lady uses her gentle soft hands to turn my fat arm. Mum says *be brave Frank, I know you can be brave* and she kisses the top of my head and I cry and cry and cry.

Afterward it's not so bad because I'm bundled back into the white bedsheets sling and Mick zooms me to my little cubicle to wait to see my pictures. My face bounces back at me from glass windows and it's all damply streaked with crying but Mick doesn't say anything about that. He tells me about his car which is named Marvin and is older than Dad. Our car doesn't have a name and when I tell Mick that, he says Marvin is his baby even though he's got four grown-up children and a dog named Winston.

2   15   14   5   19

THE DOCTOR SHOWS me my X-ray and the inside of my arm is cloudy gray with shock-white lines and one of them is torn through the middle. The bones are reaching for each other and the sharp-cut edges should fit together in a ghost jigsaw but they're all jaggedy and wrong and Halloweeny. I really want to show Ahmed and Jamie the X-ray because my arm's definitely broken and that is definitely excellent. When Sam broke his arm he had a cast wrapped in different-colored stripes and it was rough and heavy and we wrote our names with felt tips and scratched the ink into drawings and because he couldn't play soccer he got to referee all our games.

I choose bright blue for my cast and Mum shields her eyes and says *you'll blind us all* and we look at each other and laugh but then I'm worried because I chose blue for Max really but I remember Rhoda's vest. I want to change my mind but the plaster cast man is ready with rolls and rolls of blue bandages. I've had two chalky white pills that the doctor gave me and my arm aches a bit but on the very edge of all the thoughts I have. The plaster cast man wraps my arm up licketysplit and his hands are careful and it's neater than a Christmas present and very blue and maybe it's too blue and I worry.

The laughitis doctor doesn't glue my head together because she's been called away to An Emergency which means that all the doctors went swish out of cubicles and did a funny running walk to a room with a big angry sign on the door telling patients never ever to go in unless you're The Emergency.

A nurse named Sadie fixes my head with a gloopy goo and not a glue stick. It hurts but I say it doesn't because Sadie says I look brave and I want to believe her. Mum looks a little green and asks if I mind if she makes a super-quick call to Dad and I think she might be sick so I say *go please go* because I hate sick. Sadie looks at my cut and says I'll probably have a scar but that girls will like it a lot. I don't really care if girls will like my scar because I don't play with any girls and it's Jamie and Ahmed and Sam who will really want to see my glued egg.

Sadie asks me lots of questions about Minecraft and sports and all the things I like and I tell her because she's kind and when she smiles she means it. She asks what I want to be when I grow up and I say *I want to be a detective* even though I've never even thought of that before but I like it right away because detectives can crack codes. Sadie says *that's a great choice* and asks if my mum and dad are detectives. I laugh at the thought of my mum in a hat like the one Sherlock Holmes wears and carrying a magnifying glass. I tell Sadie that my dad makes computer codes and my mum was an artist but she's not really one anymore and then my voice gets lost. Sadie says that being an artist sounds *so fun* and that she loves to paint when she's not gluing up people's heads. She asks what Mum likes to paint and I try to describe the whirly shapes and splashes of color and starbright swirls of sky and Sadie seems to understand.

Next she asks about brothers and sisters and I nearly choose to say *no* but then I say *Max*. I tell her about his flapping and melting and noises and biting and the new school. Sadie asks what Max likes to do and I think that's a strange question so I answer a bit slowly about *Goodnight Moon* and the washing machine and drawing but not talking and Sadie nods and asks if Max has a favorite movie. It's *Cars* and *Cars 2* and she's all excited and sparkly and says those are her little boy Bobby's favorite movies too and he's five too and his favorite thing ever is Spider-Man. She asks if Max likes some other movies that Bobby likes and I say he does because he does and then she shows me a picture on her phone and her little boy is just like any little boy with curly blond hair and a superhero T-shirt. So I ask her if he's like Max and she says not in the way I mean but they like the same movies and she's sure other things too because they're both little boys starting school. I think that doesn't mean anything and they're not the same.

Sadie finishes sticking my head back together and says I can go home soon but not to school today. Mum is still talking to Dad to tell him about my jigsaw bones so I make Sadie promise she will tell Mum I have to go home with her and not to Wolverton Juniors. I'll show Year Six my cast tomorrow.

Mum gets a prescription for me which is a piece of paper that we swap for more chalky white pills to stop my arm from buzzing and then we can go go go. Another nurse smiles when we walk out and says to Mum *see you soon* and I ask Mum why and Mum ruffles my hair and says the nurse means when I come back to get my cast off.

Walking feels funny because my bright blue cast is heavy and drags me down like a sucking swamp and I can smell it too. It smells like paint and dust and something sharp but I can't find its name. I ask Mum what time it is because I'm suddenly starving and I tell her I'm hungrier than a hungry hippo and I could eat a horse. Mum says she's not sure if we have any horses in the freezer but then you never know and she chuckles.

She looks at her watch which has hands that can light up in the dark without even pressing a button and says it's lunchtime and we can go to McDonald's but *shhh don't tell your father*. I am full of a balloon stretching with happiness inside me but I still have room for two Big Macs and a strawberry milkshake. It's funny only eating with one hand because I haven't ever thought that I eat with two hands and I'm not even using a knife and fork for my burger. I still make a mess and get some splotchy red ketchup on my blue cast but Mum says never mind and calls me a *mucky pup*. We play tic-tac-toe on the napkins and I show Mum YouTube videos on her phone and when I think she's going to say we have to leave she gets me an apple turnover and I win seven games of Hangman in a row.

23 15 18 47 25

WHEN WE DRIVE home I am full and warm and I feel
better than if I was a wildboy with rabbit in his belly and a
firewarm cave in the woods. Mum goes slowly around all
the bends so my arm doesn't get jolted and jiggled about
and I'm glad because I'm thinking about my X-ray and
how maybe if I move too fast then the bones will slide right
past each other. Sadie said they would knit together which
I thought was a funny way of saying it because my bones
are not woolly. Sadie also told me that teeth are bones and I
look at mine in the side mirror and all the usual little white
squares in my mouth are suddenly wrong and I don't want
my tongue to touch them. Then Mum wonders how Max's
first day was and her lips smile but her eyes are tight with
worry and I forget about my boneteeth and worry too.

Mum runs her hands over the blue silk scarf wrapped
around her short hair. Mum used to have really long hair
that ran in a black river all the way down her back. She
brushed it so hard that it crackled and shone and when she
was thinking hard she would twist it up into a coil above

her head and let it fall down in a silky waterfall. Max used to love her long hair and he would whimper and cry if he couldn't put his hands in it and run his fingers through every hair and wrap it around them. He wasn't always gentle, and when Mum told him no he would melt and scream until he could soothe himself again with the strands. A few months ago Mum went to the hairdresser and came back with her hair chopped short and it was like a whole new person was in our kitchen. Max didn't eat for three days afterward and he kept pulling sharply on the new hair as if he had to check what was missing and it hurt her. So now Mum wears a scarf or a bandana wrapped up tight and Max is starting to forget.

Dad opens the front door for us and gives his long low impressed whistle-wow at my arm and at my head. He holds me by the shoulders and takes a good look at my egg and says *and did they tell you what to do if your head falls off? But seriously, thanks for another day off work, I owe you one* and I giggle and Mum hits him with the paper bag of chalky white pills.

Max is in the living room sitting on the floor and he's wearing just his spacepants and his gray-and-yellow-striped T-shirt. Max wears spacepants because he is scared of the toilet and the hiss of the flush and the water that appears from nowhere. Max doesn't call them spacepants and they're really a diaper but they have planets printed on them and they're for bigger boys than babies. I don't tell anyone about them. Max is looking at his *Goodnight Moon* and watching TV and using one hand to squash a ball that looks like an eyeball. I bought that ball at the school fair but not for Max so it's mine but I don't say anything.

I look at Max's face because then I think I'll know what happened at school. His skin is so pale it glows ghostly but that's Max and his eyes are dark with bruisey tiredness under them but that's Max too. There are no actual real bruises or angry red raw teeth marks on his hands so I think it might have been okay.

I say *hi Max I broke my arm when I fell off that chair. I've got a blue cast and it doesn't hurt that much and there's glue holding my whole head together.* Max sideways looks with the corners of his tired eyes and he puts a finger in his mouth and then touches my cast and I think *gross* but I don't move just yet. I am glad it's not too bright because Max wouldn't touch it if it was because the color would burn his skin. Max seems to feel colors with his whole body and doesn't just see them with his eyes like me. I think that's why he won't eat them at all, ever.

How was school Max? I ask and I say *was it good?* and I do a big smile or *was it bad?* and then I do a silly cross frowny face. Max laughs and he puts his licky fingers on my face and pulls it into a frown again but he's not really answering my question. I get his thumbs-up thumbs-down picture cards and say *choose!* but he just giggles and grabs my face again and his dribbly fingers knock my glued egg and I shriek like it's cracked. Max hooks his fingers in his ears and his jaw goes **CLAMP** and twitchy and he's gone far away into another world so I get up off the floor which is hard to do with one arm working and the other arm not. I slump on the sofa and I put the TV on with the sound down low and for once Max curls up beside me and watches with half an eye.

Mum comes in and says how happy she is to see me and Max together like that and she tells us that we're not just her world but we are her universe and her space and her stars and her sky and her galaxy and her cosmos too just like she always says. She says she's scared to give me a cuddle because I'm all messy and falling apart at the seams and I might crumble to dust but she's joking and she cups my face in her hands and gives me a cinnamon hug and it's because she's made my favorite cookies. They're in the kitchen and they're shaped like different dinosaurs except they got too big in the oven so they're puffy fat beasts with stumpy legs and wobbly spikes. I'm still filled up with apple pie and milkshake and burgers but I eat a cookie because she made them just for me.

After Max has had his French fries and not had his bath and is wrapped up cozytight in his bed Mum shows me a green notebook with his name on it and says it's a journal that his teachers write in every day. It's not written like Max is saying it all which I like and I read about how Max played an alphabet game on an iPad and chose a xylophone from the choosing box and found his name on his peg. No he didn't I think and I say *he can't read*. Mum shrugs and says *he's taken it in somehow and it's only three letters so at least we made that easy for him*. And I sit in the kitchen where the floor is shining clean after my sticky head blood and I sulk because if Max can do these things there then why doesn't he do them here and just be a normal brother.

19 23 5 34 20 48

THE NEXT MORNING Mum wants me to stay at home with her and she says she'll make the sofa into a nest of pillows and comforters and the TV can be all mine at any volume but that's not true because Max will come home at twelve sharp. She says *we can have a morning just us two, I'd like that.* And then her voice goes a bit funny but I've just seen myself in the bathroom mirror and my forehead is smudgy with a blue bruise that's blooming like a flower and there's a split of red with dribbles of glue meshing its edges and I think *cool.* I want to go and show my arm and my bruised egg to Ahmed and Jamie and Sam.

So I wheedle *please please please I want to be in Year Six* and Mum dithers about and she's *just not sure* but then Max squawks a parrot sound and she says *fine fine fine* and disappears to find out why he's being a bird. I get dressed but I don't have a Year Six sweater because the doctor cut it off and I find one from last year which doesn't have anything on the back. I put it in my drawer and squash it down under my pajamas and socks. I put on my polo shirt and it's hard to get my arm through the armhole, much harder than I thought it would be and it makes me hot and bothered so I definitely definitely don't want to wear my old sweater now and I don't think I could even get it on anyway and I don't want Mum to dress me because I'm not a baby. I go downstairs wearing my polo shirt and Mum says *where's your sweater Frank?* I tell her and she says *wear your one from last year* but I say it's lost.

I can't bike to school because of my arm so I think I'll have to walk on my own while everyone else shoots past. But when I leave the house Ahmed and Jamie are waiting at my gate and they look at my weird blue arm and they poke it with their fingers. Jamie taps it and says *awesome* and he makes the word really long and low so I know he's impressed. Ahmed gives me a bag of candy from his mum because she thinks breaking your arm deserves a treat. I share them with Jamie and Ahmed even though they're for me. They're all different flavors and some of them are so sour that they make our mouths pucker. We stick our tongues out to see if they've wrinkled up and the candy has painted them rainbow colors instead and Jamie's is bright purple and he looks so funny trying to see it that we can't stop laughing and all of a sudden we're late for school.

Our new teacher is Mrs. Havering and she doesn't say anything about us being late. She smiles at me which I didn't think Mrs. Havering ever did because she's as strict as a teacher from the olden days and there's a rumor she keeps a wooden cane in her desk to smack at any child who talks when she says *quiet* in a voice that's speckly with ice. She smiles again when she sees my arm and my head and I remember about teeth being bones and hers are gray. Mrs. Havering says *Frank, it's nice to have you here* and she lets me sit with Jamie even though Eric Morris told me last year that Mrs. Havering never lets friends sit together *fact.*

7 15 12 4 5 14 29 18 1 20 9 44

WE HAVE MATH for my first lesson in Year Six. I like math because you can be wrong or you can be right and I get it right. Sums are codes and you can crack them and I am the code maker and the code breaker. I haven't broken the arm I write with so I write my name **FRANK** as neat and tidy as I can on my brand-new exercise book that smells like wood and glue, but it slopes down the cover and away from me. I whizz through my worksheets and when they're finished I start even bigger sums from my new textbook that cracks like a whip when I first open it. I doodle numbers in the margins and make them as high as I can but they're not high enough because numbers never end.

After we've finished math we have art. We're going to learn about Leonardo da Vinci and Mrs. Havering tells us he was an artist *and* an inventor and he drew the plans for a helicopter hundreds of years before we had the technology for them and *how amazing is that?* She puts some pictures up on the whiteboard. One of them I know, it's the *Mona Lisa* and it lives in France and it's in one of my books at home. Another is an old drawing of a man with one head but four arms and four legs and everyone is giggling and being stupid because the man isn't wearing any clothes. Mrs. Havering lets people laugh all they want and she just stands at the front waiting and I keep thinking that they'll laugh the lesson away but after a few minutes boredom drains their voices away. Then Mrs. Havering says *some people say these paintings show us a pattern that explains the design of the whole universe.*

My head snaps up lightning fast because patterns are found in codes and that's how you crack them. My codes unlock words and sums and sometimes feelings but they can't unlock the universe because that's impossible. The universe is vast and black and random and bigger than forever and we're all just tiny specks floating inside it. I am staring at Mrs. Havering and I'm waiting for her to laugh an icy laugh and say it's all a mistake, a joke, a trick for making her wait so long to start her lesson.

But she doesn't.

A pattern that explains the design of the whole universe.

I'm leaning forward on my chair, tipping it onto two legs in the way they tell you not to or you'll slip and hit your chin on the desk and bite through your lip or break your arm exactly like I did yesterday but I don't care. I can feel my heart thump-thumping in my chest. *A code that explains the design of the whole universe.* It feels like magic, something that makes the universe make sense and every-thing that's swirling all around me fit into place.

Then Mrs. Havering speaks again. She says it's called *the golden ratio* and it's some measurements and numbers. A mathematical formula that creates proportions that can be seen throughout the universe, and that some artists use it to make their paintings as beautiful as possible. *Pleasing to the eye.* She shows us a picture of it:

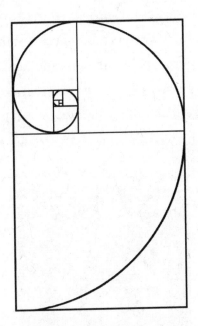

All the breath inside me hisses out again in a disappointed wheeze. It isn't what I thought it would be. Art isn't a pattern I can crack, I can't find a little chink in the sequence to dig down into and burst the meaning free. This pattern doesn't mean anything at all. I write down *golden ratio* in my exercise book and it just sits there, flat and still. Real codes leap and rattle and jump on the page when you start to solve them and explode when you crack them.

Mrs. Havering is tapping the board. She's still talking about art, about Leonardo da Vinci making this perfect picture of a man and the *Mona Lisa* using *the golden ratio*. She says all the proportions of the pictures are as perfect as possible so they're as beautiful as possible to the human eye but it doesn't look like it to me. She tells us that these measurements are found all across the universe, in the shape of our ears, of flowers and pinecones, the curve of an egg, the measurements of our arms and legs, the whorls of a snail's shell, the swirl of a hurricane seen from space, the lines of a spiral galaxy. They link space and nature and us. She shows us the *Mona Lisa* with the golden ratio on top:

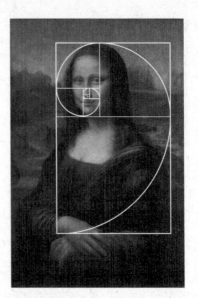

We get to use the computers to look up Leonardo da Vinci and I Google *the golden ratio*. A thousand images rush from the screen into my brain and there's a violin and an elephant's tusk and Sonic the Hedgehog and the Apple logo and the center of a sunflower and a spiral galaxy.

Now I can see it's a pattern. I feel like I've unlocked a secret code that threads itself through everything. I run my finger along the lines on the screen and look at this pattern that repeats and echoes through the universe. I feel like I've been lifted up and whirled into space. The swirl of the galaxy is dotted with stars that are salt-sprinkled into curves that spin into the blueblack ink of the infinite night sky. I print a picture of the galaxy and one that shows the golden ratio and put them in my pocket where they nestle like a secret.

3 18 1 32 11 19

AT RECESS EVERYONE gathers around me in the playground and I'm in the middle of red sweaters and excited
faces and I think *awesome* in my head in the same way as
Jamie said it. Everyone likes the blue of my arm and the
blue of the bruise creeping down from under my hair.
They rub the roughness of my cast and ask me if it hurts. I
shake my head no but I do tell them about the crunchcrack
when it broke and they love that part. *Can we sign it can we
sign it can we sign it?* Noah chants and he's already holding
a fat black pen like a sword ready to fight to mark me first.
So Year Six draws cats and faces and Minecraft pigs and
creepers and tries out graffiti writing and my cast is a blue
blur of art. I push back my hair so everyone can see my
glued-up head and Ahmed says will it scar and I nod like
it's no big deal but inside I'm a blazing bright firework and
the crowd goes *ooo*.

How'd it happen? says Sam and I want to tell a story
that's not about shouting and kitchen chairs and is about
a wildboy and a swinging vine but before I can Noah says

it was probably his weirdo brother and *he's a loony from the loony bin* and *have you seen his stroller?* Noah uses the word the boys in the park used and then another one that's different but the same and then he says Max should be sent away to a loony bin. He pulls a face that's dribbly and his eyes crisscross and his cheeks are puffed like a baby baboon and he looks nothing like Max but I know that's who he's being.

And my head is buzzing just like my arm did and bright shots of raging light are bouncing and spinning through my brain and I am red-hot liquid with a boy's skin on top and it's bubbling and soon it'll start pouring from my eyes and ears and mouth and I'll be a puddle of sparks and lava. Sam is watching me and Noah is still laughing at his own stupid face and I haven't said anything at all because if I open my hot mouth then the liquid will pour out and I'll be gone.

The red sweaters are trickling back into other corners of the playground to play soccer and jump rope and tag. Then Ahmed says *shut up Noah* and Jamie says *yeah, don't be like that* and Sam shoves Noah on the shoulder harder than friends shove each other even in soccer and Noah says the same sweary thing Dad said to a man from a church when they offered to cure Max with special prayers. Noah calls Max all the words he shouldn't and he remembers the too-big stroller and stupid *Goodnight Moon* and the noises Max makes and the flap-bounce-bop rhythm of his walk.

Jamie and Ahmed and Sam clench their fists in tight knuckled circles and they fight for Max and they swipe and kick and roar against Noah and puffed-cheek faces and awful names and words that make Mum cry and I'm still standing with one arm leadheavy with cracked bones and then the rest of me is cracked too and I can hear it happening inside me louder than my jigsaw arm snapping and louder than what is right beside me. I walk away with my mouth clamped closed but the hot seeps out from my cracks anyway and I can feel lava tears on my cheeks because I've said nothing at all.

5 13 16 20 25

AHMED AND SAM and Jamie walk with me when the last bell rings and they're full of fight and excited words even though they've all got detentions tomorrow and Mrs. Havering is fiery furious. She said *what is the **meaning** of this, boys?* and I knew the answer but not the answer she meant. No one said anything about Noah and Max because we won't tattle so Mrs. Havering put all the fighters on a list for litter picking tomorrow at lunchtime. I wasn't fighting so I don't have to stab Coke cans with a metal stick and chase fluttering potato chip bags already picked up by the wind.

Ahmed and Jamie and Sam tell me they won't have Noah on their team in PE soccer or playground soccer ever again and that he's out of line and they'll tear him up into little pieces but I am already in a thousand million black flecks and I want them to do it to me instead. I don't say anything because I didn't before and I can't unlock my mouth now and I feel so empty except for a burning ball of something that pulses in my stomach. Ahmed and Jamie and Sam think I am silent and sad and furious and they are right but they are wrong too because it's not for Noah and it's not even for Max. It's for me.

We go to the Wilderness after Sam goes home and Ahmed and Jamie shout into the sky but the trees feel like they're pressing in on me and I can't join in. I don't feel wild today and I don't write a 6 in the dirt.

I drag my feet into the house. Mum says hello and I nod and then she says Max had a wonderful day at school and that we should be proud and she's bursting with happiness. She wants to celebrate but we can't go out and she can't cook Max's favorite dinner because he always has the same one so she says she'll buy Max a little something and she'll make me lasagna which is my favorite. I shake my head no and I want to run as far away as my skinny stick legs can take me.

Max is with Angelique because it's a Tuesday and she says *hello Frank you look like you've been through a war* and I nod yes but I don't say it. *Cat got your tongue?* asks Angelique and offers me thumbs-up or thumbs-down pictures and she laughs nicely but I don't take one because it's a joke.

Max is tipping a tube of sparkly water back and forth back and forth very close to his face but he is listening and he gets up in a little bunny hop and he holds out the tube to me. I reach out for it and then Max jumps like he's just remembered something important and he has because he gives me the picture of the sparkly tube and then holds out his hand. Angelique is suddenly smiling and she says *he's got it, I think he's got it that boy*. I give Max the card and he makes a song with no words and passes the toy. I take it and I can see the glitter swirling like a starry storm and Max is still watching it and he still wants it so I give it back when he hands me the card and I say *thank you* with my hands like Angelique does and then I go to my bedroom. I can hear Angelique telling Mum about Max using the cards and the pride in Mum's voice makes the air around me shimmer. But I can't make any codes and I don't come out for lasagna and I can't make sense of anything at all.

Mum puts her head around my door and asks me if I'm not feeling well and I nod yes because I feel sick right down in the pit of my stomach where that ball of shame burns.

2   18   15   20   8   5   47

IT USED TO be different before Mum and Dad had Max. I didn't have the same swooping stomach and knotty worry and burning shame before he arrived.

I was five and he was hours, minutes and seconds when they brought him home from the hospital. He gave me a present and it was a red plastic motorcycle that I'd wanted forever and ever. It was nestled in his lap but it wasn't really from him and Mum and Dad said *say hello to your little brother* and I wanted the motorcycle so badly that I could feel it in my hand already but I didn't want to talk to the fat baby sitting in a car seat because he couldn't understand and he didn't feel like my brother one tiny bit. Mum told me that he'd change, that he'd get bigger and be my biggest fan and we could share games and toys and secrets together.

But when I was eight and Max was three he wasn't sharing my games or toys or secrets and he wasn't being the little boy Mum promised he'd be. We were in our living room and I was watching quiet TV and Max was on his hands and knees rocking backward and forward and looking at his *Goodnight Moon* and humming and not looking at any of us. Mum put her head in her hands and cried and cried and cried because she'd had a letter from the doctor that they'd been on a special trip to see and she hated what it said about Max even though the doctor had said it at the appointment but this *made it official.*

She said to Dad *we wanted him so much we tried so hard for him and he's so far away.* Dad's voice was strange and tough and sad but he said *well we still want him and he's here and he'll keep getting closer and closer.* And he read the piece of paper and he said *Max is ours and he is Max and he's just as smart as any little boy.* All his words wobbled a bit. Then he ripped up the piece of paper just like Max likes to do and Max came running over on his chubby baby legs to join in and then we all ripped up the doctor's letter into a million billion little pieces and Max was still just the way he'd always been.

I never read the letter before it became snow and dust but Mum sat me down and talked to me about it. She said *Max is autistic* and the word didn't mean anything to me so it hung between us empty in the air. Mum said it means Max sees and feels the world differently than me and her and Dad and Granny M and Jamie and Ahmed and it's like he's wearing different glasses that filter things like sounds and light and color so they stream into his brain in a way we don't understand. And all I could think about was the Wizard of Oz and the Emerald City and taking off the greenglass glasses to see that everything was different colors after all and was Max in Oz or was I? Mum said *it means he might need extra help with some things but he'll be good at other things too just maybe in a different way* and she kept saying *different* until it started to sound funny. Mum stroked my cheek and said *he might not understand the way the world works sometimes.*

I looked at Max slapping the floor with his hand and giggling and I thought about being different and the way grown-ups speak and I said *I don't understand the world either.* Mum smiled a tired smile with only her mouth and said *me too, Frank, me too.* And then she held me tight and she said Max was my brother and how I might have to be brave for him sometimes. Then she asked me what Max and I were and I chanted back that *we weren't just her world but we were her universe and her space and her stars and her sky and her galaxy and her cosmos too* and she didn't let go.

21 14 9 22 5 18 19 34

THE NEXT DAY at school I feel sick every time I see Noah and every time I think about what he said and what I didn't say. I don't play soccer at lunchtime because of my arm and I'm supposed to be the referee but I mutter something about a headache and I know Ahmed doesn't believe me but he sits with me on the sidelines and shares secret candy from his pocket.

When I get home I don't say anything to Mum even when she asks me questions and the main one is *are you all right?* over and over. I watch stupid TV that's so stupid I fall asleep and when I wake up in a hot warm tangle of blankets and heat I hear scratchy scribble noises in the hall and it's not Max because he's on the floor in front of me drawing on a piece of paper that's almost as big as him. Then Mum comes in and she's with Mark and he's got his dog Neil with him. Neil's got the best feathery fan tail that thumps from side to side which means he's happy. I stroke his velvet ears. I think that Mum and Mark will have a cup of tea and talk about art like they always do but Mum says

Mark wants to know if you'd like to go for a walk with Neil. I know that Mark doesn't want to know that but Mum has asked him to want to know that.

But I don't mind because I want to walk Neil and for him to be my wolf companion like a real wildboy would have and so I still don't talk but I nod and put on my shoes and we walk to the park. Mark lets me hold Neil's leash which is midnight blue. I wrap it around my hand and Neil pulls so it tightens against my skin but he doesn't pull so much that it hurts. Mark talks so I don't have to and he tells me about his stay-at-home job which is a designer and he explains it to me and I still don't really know what he does but I listen while he talks about galleries and prints and I don't say anything. Not one single word or syllable or letter.

Mark calls Neil *a gentle giant* and says that means he's as big as a horse but he wouldn't hurt a fly. I say *I didn't think horses hurt flies anyway* and then I realize I've said it from my mouth and not in my head and it only took a stupid joke and a huge dog and how ridiculous is that.

I feel better now that I've opened my mouth and spoken but I don't feel better about Noah and the fight at all. I scuff my stupid sneakers that don't have high tops or colored laces and I dig the toes into a heap of leaves. Mark looks at me and I know he can tell that there are more words triptrapping their way up through my throat to jump from my mouth and so I let them.

We talk about everything and something and nothing at all. When we are silent it is calm and my voice isn't shouting inside. When we do talk I tell Mark about soccer and school and my golden ratio code that can be seen throughout the whole universe and then suddenly I tell him about Noah and the fight that I didn't fight. I feel lighter when the words are out and the deep seeping shame inside me doesn't go away but its red-hot color fades a little bit. Mark doesn't say anything until he says *I've got a Max*. And he tells me he's got a brother named Stephen who is the same as Max but forty-two and different in a lot of other ways but Stephen likes spinning and hates noises but not all noises and he goes out on trips with a group of other grown-ups and he likes museums and bowling and the movies when they turn the volume down and the lights up.

Mark shows me a picture on his phone and Stephen is looking sideways and showing his teeth but not smiling just like Max does when someone says *smile* but he isn't happy. He is all skinny angles and his hands are by his sides and I know they are frozen mid-flap. I ask where Stephen lives. Mark says Stephen lives in a house with lots of other people who need extra help but he goes to Mark's mum and dad every weekend and once a month Mark drives up to take Stephen for a pizza. Stephen doesn't come to Mark's house because he wouldn't like the change or the journey or the pizzas.

I think about Max in a house he doesn't know and people who don't know to put Quavers on his plate and who turn the TV up too loud. I think about Max being hundreds of miles away, just a speck in the distance far away from me and I feel a prickle of something in my stomach. And then I think about living with Max just the two of us and him banging his head on the floor and screaming and Mum not being there to find an emergency bubble tube and a cushion and to put a cool hand on his forehead and say *finished finished finished look at these bubbles Maxy* and my stomach feels even stranger.

6 1 13 9 12 25

THE NEXT DAY at school I don't look at Noah at all. Mrs. Havering stands at the front of the classroom and stretches her spine upward until she seems almost like a giant and I know she's going to say something important. She turns and writes on the board and when she steps backward I can read the words **FAMILY TREE** printed in her neat script. Mrs. Havering pulls the corner of her shirt collar so that it's perfectly pointed and then she tells us about the Big Year Six Project. She asks Kai what a family tree is and he jokes that it's a tree that you have in your garden that belongs to your family and Noah sniggers even though it's a dumb joke. Every time I hear Noah I feel a hot burning anger that bubbles with my own shame at not saying a word when he was saying all his terrible ones.

Mrs. Havering says *that's not quite right* and then Jamie says *it's your family history.* Mrs. Havering smiles a real smile and says *that's exactly right.* She draws a tree with quick strokes of her pen on the whiteboard and it's only a few swipes of ink but Mrs. Havering is a good drawer. Then she writes the names **ALEXANDER MARSHALL** and **MARYA PETROVA** at the top and draws a line between them and lines down falling from them toward the branches. She says *these are my great-grandparents* and then she puts little crosses by their names and explains that this symbol means they're dead. It seems such a tiny little mark for something so big.

As she draws she talks about each name and the person behind it. Her grandfather was an engineer on the railways and his mother, Marya, came from Russia a hundred years ago or more. Her sister is a doctor who lives in Australia. Her brother is a writer and he lives in England and has three children—*here they are on the branch below, Molly, Harriet and Zach.* Mrs. Havering has a husband named Richard and a grown-up son named Jason and he's got a baby on the way so Mrs. Havering draws a little twig down from Jason and his wife's branch but the baby isn't born yet so she doesn't write a name. She pauses in the blank space next to Jason's name for just a flicker of a moment and she opens her mouth and then closes it again without saying a word.

Noah is sniggering again because Mrs. Havering has written her real first name on the tree and it's Agnes, but everyone else is mesmerized by the quick flicks of her pen and the history emerging from the branches.

Mrs. Havering tells us that our Big Project this year will be to make trees of our own families. She tells us we'll have to research our families and ask our parents and grandparents, and even great-grandparents if anyone has any, all about our family histories. She says we have to write biographies with as much information as we can possibly find out about each of our family members, including parents and siblings. She smiles and says we might find out new and exciting things about people we thought we knew well and that we should find photographs or draw pictures too.

Ahmed rolls his eyes and mutters something darkly about having too many relatives to fit even on an oak tree. His house is always full of sisters and brothers and cousins and second cousins and aunts and uncles and grandparents and it definitely seems like he'll have more work to do than me because I only have Max and Mum and Dad and Granny M and Mum's brother Dan and Dad's brother Simon and their parents but we never see them because they're a million miles away in Scotland where Dad grew up. Simon still lives there but in a big city and not in a teeny village with only one store and no buses or trains like my grandparents. We used to visit them in the village but Max doesn't like being away from home and now they're too old to come and see us. Mum's brother lives in America which is so cool but we never get to see him either because it's even farther than Scotland and he says he only comes back for weddings and funerals. I don't know how to write about our family and the history of Max and I don't want Noah to read his life and use those awful words.

Mrs. Havering gives us new notebooks which have lined pages and blank pages and bright red covers. She says we have to record our research in them and that we'll build a Family Forest at the end of the spring term. The Big Year Six Project isn't the same every year because last year they had chicks that they hatched from eggs and made scientific notes about their development and now they live in a coop in the caretaker's garden, and I'm disappointed we're not doing that instead. I like to go and see them scratching at the dirt and clucking softy to each other and sometimes the caretaker gives out eggs to take home and their yolks are like suns. I remember when I was in Year Two that the Year Sixes did family trees because they made great big trees from cardboard and tissue paper and paint and lots of other things too. Then they made the Family Forest in the auditorium and we all walked through it.

2 5 6 15 18 34

WHEN I GET home I take out the red notebook and leaf through its blank pages. Mum's brother and Dad's parents and his brother Simon are too far away to interview in person and my stomach feels knotty when I think about doing it over the phone because I don't really know them at all. I write their names down anyway because I have to fill in the tree even if it's nothing more than names scribbled on a branch. I only have Mum, Dad, Max and Granny M to talk to in person and I can't even ask Max because he's still working on swapping cards for toys.

I ask Mum about her life story and she seems a little surprised. She laughs and says that I know she was an artist and that she still is, she supposes. Her hands flutter to the bright silk of her headscarf as she talks. I start writing and let her voice scribble itself onto the pages of my notebook.

She grew up near here with Granny M and Grandpa and he died when I was three. *He never got to meet Max* she says thoughtfully. She met Dad at the university when they were both still teenagers and young and carefree. When he got his first job they went on a trip to Venice to celebrate, just packed up and drove to the airport and spent the whole weekend eating pasta and sailing up and down canals in special long boats called gondolas. She saw lots of famous art there and when she came home she painted the first painting that she ever sold. She painted the universe in ways people had never seen it before, microcosms of dust particles and spinning lights tracking across an infinite space reduced onto a canvas. *Spiral galaxies* I think suddenly, and Mum keeps talking while that thought bubbles in my head.

More and more people asked for her art, more people than she could possibly paint for and she and Dad bought a house with a studio in the attic and then I came along and when I was a tiny baby she would put me in a bouncing chair and paint the universe again but it looked very different to her now that I was in it. And then Max came along and he wouldn't sit in that bouncing chair without screaming and screaming so she put down her paintbrushes and she's been meaning to pick them up again for the longest time and then her voice trails off and she says very quietly *I'm just too tired and busy now, Frank.*

And in that moment I hate Max.

19 20 1 18 29 4 21 48 49

MARK COMES AROUND that evening to ask if I'd like to go for a walk with him and Neil. He has a cup of tea with Mum first and then chats to Dad when he gets home from work and I'm impatiently hopping from foot to foot waiting for them to finish while Max tries to stick his finger in Neil's ear and I catch his wrist to stop him and he shrieks.

When we get outside, I ask Mark what spiral galaxies are made of and I think that he's a grown-up so maybe he might even know though I know by now that grown-ups just pretend to understand a lot of the time. He runs his hand through his hair and throws a tennis ball for Neil who immediately tries to swallow it whole. Mark gets out his phone and types for a few moments and I see the same pictures that I looked at popping up on the screen. *Still interested in the code of the universe then?* he asks. I nod.

Mmm he says. *Well spiral galaxies follow the golden ratio proportions. I think they've got a flat disc of stars in the middle and arms full of stars that look like the spirals you can see in those pictures.*

I look at him and he pulls the tennis ball out of Neil's slobbery mouth and throws it again even though Neil is much more interested in eating the ball than chasing it.

The arms full of stars look brighter because they're bigger and younger than the stars in the middle.

Mark throws Neil's ball into the light that's melting slowly from the sky. *You know what's really cool* he says and I don't think anything could be cooler than spiral galaxies but I shake my head and say *what, what's cool?*

We're all made of star dust. Everything in our bodies began with a huge bang in space billions of years ago. It's true, promise. Stars are born and they die, just like us. They're still being born and dying right now. And when they die, they throw off the stuff they're made of and it works its way through space and into us. Our bodies are made from the remains of stars and huge explosions in our galaxies. Everything in us first came from space. That's pretty cool, isn't it?

We're made of star dust.

It's the coolest thing in the universe.

6 12 25 9 14 7

AHMED AND JAMIE and I make a rope swing in the Wilderness. We find loops and loops of twisted blue rope in Jamie's garage and we borrow it to tie to the thickest and highest branches of a tree. Ahmed ties fat knots along it so that we can hold on tight and wrap our legs around the rope like monkeyboys and not slip and slide off into the ground. My arm is still wrapped up tight in itchy plaster but now it's gray and crumbling at the edges and for a moment I'm worried my bones will crack again but I can still curl my arms around the rope and I soar through the air like a bird.

I feel feather tips nudging underneath my skin waiting to burst through because I'm an eagle and a kite and a hawk and I swoop through the mud-scented wind looking for prey. I'm an astronaut, weightless in space. I am high above the world that holds Noah and his words that snag like thorns and away from Max's special things and meltdowns and screams. We swing until the sun has melted away and our cheeks are whipped red by the wind as we fly and I can almost stretch out my fingers and touch the stars that made us.

Afterward we write 6 and 1 and 10 in the dirt just like always.

6   9   24   5   4

IT'S TUESDAY AND Mum and I go to the hospital after
school to get my cast cut off. Noah's name still shines
N O A H in the middle of all of the other Wolverton art
and I can feel the letters have dripped through the cast into
me and I can't get rid of the way he made me feel and the
way he made me act. He made the sick-sorry feeling that
began when I laughed at Max in the park start to spread
into my bones and wrap around them like tentacles and
they tighten whenever I see him at school.

I don't see Sadie or Mick or the laughitis doctor at the
hospital even though I look out for them. The doctor who
is going to cut my cast off isn't funny like the other one
and she doesn't tell me stories like Mick did but she has a
buzzy round saw that looks like it's from a toolbox and not
from a hospital at all. I am worried that I am in the wrong
nightmare place and this doctor will cut off my arm and
all the wormy shame that sits hot and heavy in my stomach and fills my blood will come pouring out and she will
cackle and say she's curing me from being a monster.

Then I blink and the real doctor outside of my head says the saw won't cut my skin so don't worry but that my arm will feel like it's made of nothing when the blue wrapping is gone. I'm nervous and shaky scared when the buzzing starts but she's right because the saw doesn't touch my skin and my arm floats up on its own when the cast falls away and everyone in the room laughs.

My arm is puckered like after a too-long bath except it doesn't smell like I've had a bath. I wiggle my fingers and stretch and my arm is still too light and bloodless. I look at the distance from the tips of my fingers to my grubby wrist and then to my black-stained elbow and I think about how my arm is made from stars.

Mum says my arm needs a good wash and she looks at my strange skin and makes a face. Then she takes my dirty plaster-streaked hand and I think maybe now I'm too big to hold hands but I like the smooth warmth and so I curl my fingers around hers and then we swerve right and right into McDonald's and I don't have two Big Macs but I have one and a pink-iced sugar-sprinkled doughnut which tastes like the air at a fairground.

Because it's a Tuesday Max has his session with Angelique. Dad meets us at the door because he's left work early to be with Max like he promised Mum he would. He looks at my arm and pretends to be shocked when he sees my newly naked arm and Mum and I roll our eyes at him.

My arm still feels zombieish and Angelique wants to show me what Max can do and I have spelling words to learn and Minecraft to play and Ahmed wants me to have a game of soccer in the park before it gets dark so I don't want to look at Max scramble on the floor with his cards. But Angelique is smiling like she thinks of course I'd want to see this so I say *of course*. I sit on the floor where Max is curled around his *Goodnight Moon* with his thumb running up and down the closed pages so they give a paper whisper. He has a purple mark in the dark hollow of his eye and I reach out slowly to wipe it away but it's a stained perfect circle of his own bony knuckle and I know that he has screamed and tried to hit and hit and hit the buzzing wasps out of his head.

I say *Max have you got something new to show me?* and I point to Angelique and Max looks at my hand and takes it in his and weighs my arm without its cast. Angelique kneels down and speaks with her hands and mouth and says *let's show your brother, eh?* She has three toys on the kitchen table but they're actually plastic fruit which isn't very fun. And she says *Max show me the banana* and Max sideways looks at the fruit and he ignores the pear and the apple and he gives Angelique the banana. And I say *Max give me the apple* and he looks again and puts the apple in my hand and Dad is watching and says *that boy knows his apples*. There's a beat of silence when there should be laughter and Dad rolls his eyes and says he's *wasted on us* but he gives Max a gentle high five and Max shows us he knows what a pear is too and then we dance to a pocket full of posies and we all fall down.

Mum goes to bed early that night because she says she's very tired from our trip to the hospital and Dad puts Max to bed and I don't think Mum can possibly sleep through all the shrieks but she doesn't get up.

4 15 7

MARK COMES TO the house the day after my blue cast is
gone. He sees it not being there and gives me a thumbs-up.
He has a cup of tea with Mum and Max except Max has
Quavers instead and I play with Neil in the living room
and he gives me his paw and rolls over and begs and I try
to teach him to bark on command but he doesn't get it.
I want to teach him to do sums because I saw a YouTube
video where a man shouted things like *seven plus five* and
his dog would pause for a moment like it was thinking and
then bark back twelve times. Dad says the dog isn't really
counting but I don't care if he thinks that. I keep trying to
teach Neil to bark on command so we can start on numbers but it's really difficult because I don't know how to
make him bark. He sniffs where the cast is missing and I
think he can smell the stain that Noah has left inside me.
But he rubs his wiry muzzle against my hip and then Mark
comes into the room holding Neil's leash and his orange
rubber ball and says *let's take Max with us* and I say *what?*

Mum has to come too but she walks behind us. She's

pale and it looks like she's pulling her legs through mud but she's smiling in a way I don't remember. Max has his giddyup reins on so Mark walks him and I walk Neil. I am furious and I don't look at Mark because he was mine and he's ruined everything. Mark talks to Max like he'll answer and says things like *how's school?* and *what's the best thing there?* and *can you see that sparrow over there?* and he tells Max about seeing a heron last week. I don't talk to anyone and not even Neil. I don't want to share Mark and Neil with Max. Max is bouncing along in his reins and he claps and whoops and his fingers aren't in his ears and he's flapping up high.

Max likes Neil and he wants to touch him so Mark shows him how to stroke his ears and pat his head softly softly. Neil does a grumbly sigh which means he's happy and that he wants his ears scratched too. Max's fingers dance in Neil's fur and then he reaches out his hands and he says *dog* with them and Mum beams and beams and she puts her hands up to her face as if to feel her own happiness there. *That's right* I say, *dog. Good job.* And I say it like I don't mean it but I think I do because that's Max's first word.

Max wants to hold Neil's leash and so I let him and Max holds Neil and Mark holds Max. There's a chain of man and boy and dog and they stumble along unbroken and Max is making his noises louder than when he goes on the swings and there are big boys and girls and little boys and girls in the park and some of them are from school and suddenly I don't care and I say it again, *good job Max, good job.*

When we get home Mum calls Dad to tell him about Max's word and then she calls Angelique and Granny M and her brother Dan and her best friend Hazel and her other best friend Natalie. She cries when she's on the phone and she catches my eye and smiles with her whole face and my heartbeat skips because I really can't remember her face looking quite like that for a long time. She's talking really fast and saying how they should all meet up for drinks *soon because it's just been too long, hasn't it?* She still looks tired and china pale but she looks happy. Angelique is so happy that she cries on the phone too and then she says she's going to call her mum in France.

Dad makes whooping-whoop noises when he gets home and ruffles Max's black curls which he instantly hates and we're back to fingers in ears and a stiff little body screaming on the carpet. But Dad gives him a special present of colored pencils that he bought in the art store on the way home from work and when Max sees them he stops banging his head on the floor and he reaches out his hands. Then Dad calls his brother Simon and his best friend Steve and his parents far away in their map crease of Scotland where it's cold even when it's not winter and they have to wear hats in bed. News of Max's dog word is seeping out and away into the corners of the world.

After all the phone calls are finished Dad opens a bottle of champagne just like he used to do when Mum sold a painting in a gallery. He pops the cork oh-so-quietly so it doesn't upset Max because it's Max we're celebrating this time. Dad pours the bubbling honey liquid into the tall glasses that I remember from forever ago and he raises a toast to Max. Max doesn't look up from the kitchen table where he's drawing with a look of concentration on his little face, the brand-new pencils clutched in his fist. He's drawing Neil the dog and I can see the gentle spikes and tufts of his fur emerging on the paper.

I try a sip of the champagne but it's as horrible as I remember and it burns sourly on my tongue. Mum and Dad lean in close together and whisper softly while I watch Max make a portrait of his dog friend. Mum is leaning against the counter and then suddenly she slips out of view and down down down to the ground and her limbs aren't her own anymore and there's a tinkling crunch of broken glass as her champagne pools on the floor beside her. She's making an awful noise and her muscles are twitching and jerking and her face doesn't look like hers.

Dad kneels on the floor to try to stop Mum's scarf-wrapped head banging into the kitchen cabinets and his hands are sticky with blood from catching them on the champagne-soaked splinters that fan outward from Mum's body. And in a voice I haven't heard before he shouts *call an ambulance Frank and tell them your mother's having a seizure, tell them our address, tell them to come quickly.*

My fingers are shaking and I nearly can't make them work properly. When the line clicks on at the other end I tell them in a voice made of something very cold that *my mum is having a seizure and can you come quickly please?* Then Dad takes the phone from me and his blood drops and fizzes from his hands into the flood of champagne.

19 16 12 9 20 29 48 5 3 15 14 4

THE AMBULANCE ARRIVES in a frenzy of bright blinking lights that wash the kitchen walls and make Max scream. The paramedics dance around Mum's twitching body and the champagne smell rises around us. I can see the silver flash of a needle dipping into the bright blue vein of her trembling hand and then Granny M arrives and she takes Max and me away from the noises and glass and low urgent voices.

After Mum and Dad are whisked off to the hospital in the back of the ambulance Granny M goes to sweep up the glass and the blood before Max can hurt himself. I am trying to breathe and it doesn't feel right. I gasp in lungfuls of air and none of them are going to the right place and I am dizzy and sick. I keep picturing Mum laughing with her head bent close to Dad's and then the sudden shock split second when she slipped down and the moment broke. I can't sit still and I stand up and shake my arms and legs and I pace up and down and Granny M comes in and puts the TV on and then turns it off again because none of us knows what's going on. She kisses the top of my head and she says it'll *all be okay* but we both know she doesn't know that. She calls Dad a few times and just once he picks up and says that Mum's *stable* and my lungs and the air start working together again.

Granny M doesn't give Max a bath because it's not worth it and instead she cuddles him close while she gently tugs off his clothes and lifts him into his pajamas. Max sucks his fingers urgently and he looks around for Mum but he doesn't melt but he won't go to sleep either and neither will I. We all sit on the sofa huddled together and after a while I am dragged into a fitful sleep until I hear the click of the front door and see Dad helping Mum up the stairs.

The next day Granny M gets me up at the normal time even though I feel like my eyes are full of sand and I haven't slept at all. At breakfast Dad isn't wearing his work clothes and he sits opposite me and tells me that Mum had a seizure and that if it ever happens again I have to call the emergency number just like I did so well last night and tell them what's happening and give them our address in a really clear voice. He pauses to clear his throat because his own voice suddenly isn't very clear and then he tells me that Mum is *going to be okay* and *they don't think it'll happen again* because the doctors have given Mum some medicine to take every day. It might make her a bit sleepy and so we all have to be good and we all have to help her as much as possible. Max is sitting right next to me quietly sucking Quavers into a mush but Dad isn't even looking at him, he's looking at me.

19 3 18 5 1 13 9 14 7

AT SCHOOL I fall asleep at my desk and Mrs. Havering wakes me with her cool gentle hand on mine. The doctor comes to see Mum at home that evening and he gives her more pills and she swims up from sleep just long enough to smile at me when I creep into her room before bedtime. One of her hands is bandaged where she cut it on the champagne glass and there's a bruise on the back of her other hand where the hospital had to put more needles into her to stop the seizure. And I don't know what's wrong with her and no one will tell me even when I ask over and over and Dad will only say *she's going to be fine.* I just want to scream and scream and scream into space until my voice bounces off a galaxy and shatters the sky.

1 6 18 30 9 4

TWO DAYS LATER Mum is better because she's up and about and cooking and laughing and making me eat peas and opening bags of Quavers for Max and making sure we've got everything we need for school on Monday and helping us with our homework. She's excited because Max is going to start going to his spaceship school full-time. Her eyes are very bright and when I ask her whether she knew that a day on Jupiter only lasts for 9 hours and 56 minutes she takes such a very long time to answer that I think she's forgotten what I said.

Mum climbs the stairs to the rickety attic room and she's going to clean it up so she can maybe start painting again now that she'll have more free time. That means I can't go up there when Max is shouting or when I want to write the coded words of worry that are eating away my insides on the canvas. I write them in tiny pencil print that can be erased with the swish of an eraser in the back of my bright red family tree notebook instead.

Max has not once been sent home from the spaceship

school for being a hoppity handful of beans. He doesn't get into trouble like I would for doing the kinds of things he does, like throwing chairs or not sitting down when he should or humming when the teacher is speaking. Mum says she is so happy with him and how hard he works. His green notebook with letters from his teachers says that he is smart and funny and wonderful and that he can find some alphabet letters on a board without any help. Max loves his teacher and he especially loves Rhoda. She wears her vest the right way round now and Max sometimes lets himself touch it but he pulls his hand away superfast to stop the bright yellow burning him and staining his skin.

Mum is still tired but we walk with Mark and Neil most afternoons unless she's too exhausted and then Granny M comes instead. Max hasn't said anything new since *dog* but he says it with his hands each time he sees Neil. He says *dog dog dog dog dog dog dog dog dog dog dog dog dog dog dog dog dog dog dog dog dog* forever and ever until I think his hands must throb with tired and cold because he won't wear gloves but every word means he is happy.

I look at him speaking with his hands and I look at the smile that breaks his face in two when he sees Neil and I feel cold inside because all I can think about is Mum and her bright bruisey eyes and her bird bones and her falling down down down and I'm afraid. And I think that she wouldn't be so tired and so pale and so thin if it wasn't for Max waking up and shouting and Max lashing out and melting and Max not being able to just be like other children. Once Granny M comes with us even though Mum says she's not too tired but her feet are stumbly and Granny M holds Mum's hand just like she's a child all over again. She puts her head close to Mum's bird-boned face and I hear a whisper of what she says and it's that she has to tell us soon, and I think tell us *what?*

4 1 18 11 14 5 19 48

GRANNY M IS in the kitchen and she's started peeling potatoes for dinner. Mum had another seizure last week and she's too tired and fuzzy from the new drugs the doctors gave her to cook the dinner today. I didn't see the seizure so I couldn't call the ambulance but I still feel sick and icy with fear when I remember that first time I saw her terrible tumbling body twitching on the kitchen tiles and I try to shake it out of my head. Granny M squeezes my shoulder and tells me to keep my chin up and haven't I got something to do that might take my mind off it all?

I go and get my bright red notebook because it's full of snow-white pages except for Mum's story and the codes I can't scribble on the canvas upstairs. When Mrs. Havering gives us time to work on the Family Tree project I just twirl my pencil around the codes on the back pages because I don't want to write the story of Max. But today at recess I could hear Noah shouting about how he'd found out that his great-grandfather had been a hero soldier in World War II and Kai said his great-great-uncle had flown planes in the RAF against the Germans and my stomach lurched when I thought of the mostly blank pages in my book.

I sit at the kitchen table and draw a tree on one of the unlined pages and I expect it to look awful but I actually think it's good. I hold my pen tightly and swirl the nib over another page drawing spirals and squares before I ask Granny M to tell me her story starting at the beginning. When I do, she looks surprised just like Mum did and I don't think she's ever had someone ask her that question before. She takes off her apron and sits down next to me.

She tells me her parents were very poor. They were from up in the very north of the country and her father worked in the mines, deep below the earth in the darkness where he dug out coal and breathed in black air and stained his skin dark every day with the dust. He would come home with a cloud drifting up from his clothing and even when he scrubbed and scrubbed with soap and water the dust wouldn't shift and it was a part of his skin, a tattoo of his work. He would cough up great black chunks and Granny M would think that his whole lungs were coming up.

When Granny M was six and her sister was four, the mine that her father was working in exploded. The earth blew right out of the ground and the spray of black splattered across the town. Granny M was in school and she felt the ground boom beneath her feet and the teachers knew exactly what had happened. Their husbands and their brothers and their sons worked in that mine and they all ran out of the school building and raced toward the explosion. Some of the men were already staggering away but some of them were dead and some of them were trapped in the mine under the collapsing weight of the earth.

Granny M's father wasn't one of the dead but he could never work in a mine again. He was hoisted out by the men in the town and lay gasping on his back and coughing great clouds of blood-thickened black dust up from his lungs. He went to bed after that day and he didn't get up again. *I don't know if it was his body or his mind that gave up* says Granny M. *I don't think it really mattered.*

She says *that's enough for one day* and then she helps me write the names of her father and mother and puts little crosses by their names to show that they're not alive anymore. I put in the name of her sister, Sylvia, myself because we've been to visit her before. She has a thousand little glass paperweights filled with bubbles of color and I wanted to touch them more than anything but she wouldn't let children go near them. Mum held Max very tightly.

The next day we work on our projects at school. Mrs. Havering wants us to copy the stories we have so far in our red notebooks onto lined paper and illustrate them. *You're going to make books about your families* she says and she lets us all go to the art room. We traipse along the corridors and sit around the big table in the middle of the room and start to design part of our books.

Mrs. Havering has a pile of blank covers and a pile of lined sheets that we can staple inside the covers. The books will hang from the branches of the trees when we make the Family Forest in the auditorium. We're supposed to have the story of a different family member in each one, even if it's just a page and some drawings. Mrs. Havering tells us that *everyone has a story that's longer and more complex than we might ever imagine, even a tiny baby.*

I write up Mum's story neatly and stick a photo of her and Dad on the cover and I've even got some pictures of her paintings that I printed at home so I can glue them to the inner pages to show that she's an artist. Jamie sticks a photo of his mum to the cover of her story and tells us that she's a surgeon which is true and that she is a spy which definitely isn't. I get a new blank cover but I don't have a photo of my great-grandfather and I don't know what he looked like at all so I let my hand take over and when I look back at the picture I've made, it's like I'm looking at me as a grown man. Jamie gives an impressed whistle and says my drawings are always the best in the class and this one looks almost real and I burn with pride.

8   9   19   20   15   18   25

DAD AND I play some Hangman before school, except I'm not going to school today. It's the last day before the October school break and the whole of Year Six is going on a trip to the Natural History Museum. It's going to be so much better than doing another spelling test, which is what a Friday morning normally is.

Mum takes her pills every morning and evening, which she keeps in a locked box just in case Max decides he's going to eat colors today. Today she pops out some different ones and says she's got a terrible headache. I feel sick to my stomach because looking after us is making her ill and I try to be as good as gold. Max didn't sleep last night, not one tiny little bit. He bounced and jumped and squealed and I pushed my head under my pillow and scrunched my fingers in my ears until his shouts were just a wash of noise like the sea. Dad puts his arm around Mum and says that the neighbors must hate us but Mum doesn't smile and one of our neighbors is Mark and he says he likes to hear the noises of a family but he probably doesn't think that at 3 a.m. Mum rubs her face and says she's too tired to function and her head is killing her. Dad says he'll come home early from work and take Max to the swings as soon as he gets in from school so that Mum can rest all day. This isn't the routine because Dad doesn't usually go to the park and Max won't like it and so I know Mum must feel really awful. Right then, I hate Max in a fresh wave of anger. Mum puts her arms around me and I feel her jutting bird bones and she kisses the top of my curls and tells me to be good and how she wishes she could come with me to the museum because it's like looking through a thousand layers of time and history all at once.

The wind is nibbling my ears and I've forgotten my hat and Year Six gets on an old smelly bus. We don't have to wear our uniform and that makes everyone look strange. I am wearing my favorite bright yellow sweater and Jamie is wearing the same one because we bought them together last year. We planned it that way and we say we will be twins today and that no one will be able to tell us apart. Jamie is blond like pictures of angels and I'm not so we are definitely joking but Mrs. Havering calls me Jamie for fun and I think that maybe the rumors about the cane in her desk aren't true. There are rows and rows of seats on the bus so I sit with Ahmed and far away from Noah. Noah doesn't talk to us anymore and he thinks this is a bad thing for us but it's not.

Ahmed has a new game on his phone and we swipe at zombies and I'm good at it. I beat his high score and he doesn't mind because he says he doesn't play it much anyway so I pow and blast them to brains and gunk until the bus belches up to the museum. We climb down its narrow chewing-gummed stairs and clamber up gray stone steps and take clipboards and worksheets and promise to meet the teachers at checkpoints every hour and then we scatter like birds.

This place is full of bones. My lightning-white bones in my cloudy X-ray are tiny splinters compared to the ancient skeletons of beasts from forever ago that have been puzzled back together and are rising around us. I feel like a minuscule dot in the whole huge history of the world. I want to touch the bones but they make my eyes feel dizzy and I think if I reach out a hand then I'll fall so I look and look and look and this is the world a million years ago right here. I take out the little scrap of spiral galaxy that I always keep in my pocket. I can see it threading its pattern through history, through the bones and animals and plants that tower around my head. The swirlshape of a spiral galaxy spins through the curls of ammonites and the winding fronds of fossilized ferns, the arced skulls of dinosaurs and the curve of unhatched eggs.

Ahmed and Jamie want to find stuffed animals and not just look at bones and at first I think they mean toys but these are real dead animals made to look alive. There are hundreds of them sealed into glass boxes as if they might escape. They stretch and roar and graze and pounce but they're stiff and glassy-eyed and some of them have dribbles of glue on the seams clutching their skin. I think they're disgusting but Jamie presses his face into the glass and smears it with his breath so he can look closer and closer at a snarling crocodile. Ahmed tells us that crocodiles have the strongest bite of any animal in the world and Jamie wants one as a pet so he can set it on people. I look at the crocodile and its green puckered armor and its blank eyes and I feel funny because it's dead and it's in a strange glass tank with pretend plants like it's in its real world but it doesn't look right at all. I feel sorry for that crocodile.

Ahmed reads a pamphlet and tells us there's a room with loads of butterflies but I don't want to see dead bugs pinned to the wall. Ahmed rolls his eyes and says *they're alive dummy*. He shows me and Jamie the pamphlet and there's a whole tunnel that looks like a tent filled with butterflies from all over the world. The pictures show bright wings nestled in stretched-out palms. I want to hold a butterfly. We find the tent tunnel which is difficult because it's outside and Jamie and Ahmed argue about which way it is and I get distracted by a stuffed wombat because I've never seen anything like it.

In the tent the air is full of butterflies and I never knew that they could have a smell but they do. It's musty and fresh at the same time and I like it. The tent is thick with a warm heat and I roll up the sleeves of my sweater. There are big wooden troughs filled with flowers and plants and it's a lot better here than looking at the dead animals in their tanks. The butterfly keepers wander around and they say *don't touch them like that* and *they like this* and *they don't like that.* It still seems strange to be standing in a plastic tunnel outside a museum in the middle of a city with hundreds of butterflies whirling around like a velvet tornado but they have real plants and nestley places to hide. It's not their real world but I think it's getting there.

The butterflies land on me because I'm wearing bright yellow and they think I'm a flower and they do the same to Jamie. It's tickly and shivery when a butterfly walks up your arm. When one lands on my hand I look at its wings and I can see through all the colors that its wings are torn like tissue paper. When I move it flies up again and the ragged edges blur into a whirl of pattern as it swoop-swooshes to another human flower.

There are lots of Wolverton children in the butterfly room and they cup butterflies in their palms and try to take pictures before they flit away again. I see Noah throwing himself in front of the butterflies as they hunt for flowers and nectar and try to hide themselves in the green fronds of plants. His hands snatch for them and they arch away from him and flap high to the ceiling in a panic of wings. I want to tell him to stop and to leave them alone and that he has to let them do what they want or it's not fair. I don't say anything though and the butterflies don't land on him even though his top is bright orange. Noah swears and says *this place is dumb and for babies* and he stomps out and more butterflies cloud upward from the flowers. I reach out my hand and one lands on my fingertip. I grin and Ahmed takes a picture.

I bike home from school after I get off the bus back from the museum, letting the wind whip up my hair and shriek past my ears. Ahmed said he could smell when it was going to snow and that today smelled like snow. Jamie said it wasn't even really winter yet and it was too early for snow but Ahmed insisted.

The sky is dark and rippling with heavy gray clouds and I hope Ahmed's right because we could go sledding in the Wilderness like last year. Dad made my sled for a Christmas present a few years ago, and it has a horn and special lights that cast an arc-beam of light that makes the white snow glitter. Last year we stayed out until my sled's lamp was the only light left and the Wilderness was absorbed into liquid blackness and then we went home and Mum made us all hot chocolates with whipped cream and marshmallows.

I let out a whoop as I fly down the hill on my bike, my scarf rippling behind me like an airplane's banner. Because it's a school break I'm going around to Jamie's this evening to play on his new PlayStation which has a virtual reality headset which can send you anywhere in the world and I'm so excited that I don't really see what's in front of me until the lights are blinding.

3   8   1   15   19

OUR STREET IS in chaos. There is a police car and an ambulance and their lights collide in the air and throw shapes into the shadows. For one moment I'm excited because it looks like something on television and then I'm scared because this is real life and something has happened. I look desperately for someone I know, for anyone who could tell me what's happening, but all the faces are strange and the lights make them look ghostly. I start to feel afraid because the car and the ambulance aren't moving and shrieking onto another street with their sirens calling out a warning. They're still and they're parked outside our ramshackle house.

I drop my bike with a clatter and start to run up to the door but before I can open it with the key I have In Case of Emergencies I see that it's already ajar and so I start forward. Before I can go inside a huge arm presses across my chest and I'm swept off the doorstep and it feels like I'm underneath a crashing wave. I wriggle and try to get free because everything feels horribly wrong. I look up and my heart is thudding against the hand that's pushing me back.

Mark is looming above me and he says *come on Frank, step back, you can't go in there just yet.* I shout out **why not why not?** and I start to fight harder against the hold he has me in and the harder I fight the stronger he gets so I start to be like Max and I bite and I scratch and for those moments I'm a wildboy bursting his bones out of his skin.

Mark is saying something and the words drop into the air but I can't make them reach my ears because of the roaring sound in my head. And then I see Dad running in a tangled sprint of limbs and I think in a flash that he's late for taking Max to the park. He's wearing his suit straight from work and he looks wrong because Dad never runs in his suit and for a split second I want to laugh. His face is wrong too and I realize that he is crying. I've never seen him cry like this before, his whole face twisting with every sob. Not when Max is at his baddest and Mum is sobbing or when his granny died of very old age or when our ginger cat Pernikitty had to be put to sleep.

Dad is talking to one of the ambulance people and I can't hear what they're saying. I twist myself in knots trying to get free from Mark's iron arms and I see Rhoda in her bright vest. I wonder why she isn't on the school bus that's parked quietly next to our car but instead she's just holding Max's hand and Max is very quiet. There is something even more wrong with what I'm seeing but I can't fit the pieces together.

And then a question hits me and it tumbles in a shuddery rush from my mouth because I know what's wrong.

And then I ask them in a voice that screams its way out

WHERE'S MUM?

And then Dad opens his mouth but he can only speak in sobs and he is swept away by the police inside the gaping mouth of our house.

And then Mark is holding me by the shoulders and his fingers are pressing into my bones and he's saying something but I don't know what.

And then a woman in an ambulance uniform is saying something and she's pointing to me and to Max and I know we're not allowed to see what's going to happen. A radio clipped to her chest keeps making chirrupy crackles and Max jumps and I reach forward to hold his other hand.

And then a police officer with numbers stitched across his shoulders comes forward and he says something to Mark and then it's just me and Max being herded away from our front door and Rhoda is standing with the ambulance lady with a hand clamped over her mouth. I look back and I cry out for Dad, and for Mum, and Mark tells me that Dad'll be with me soon but he doesn't say anything about Mum and Mum doesn't come running like she usually does.

And then we are in Mark's kitchen which is the same shape as ours but it is clean and white and all of the mugs match because they're all white too. Neil is there and Max twists his fingers into the dog's long gray fur and even though everything is new he is okay. I am not because no one is telling me anything and I can't get enough air. I press my face against the window so I can stare out onto our flashing light-drenched street but Mark gently leads me away and makes me a cup of tea with four sugars even though I don't drink tea and Mum doesn't like us having too much sugar because it'll rot our teeth right out of our heads. He puts *PAW Patrol* on for Max and he brings out a blanket and wraps him up tightly just like Max likes. Then Mark gets an iPad and he downloads games with shapes and games with colors and games with funny little creatures blobbing about on the screen. And Max sits on the sofa curled up with his cartoons and his games and Neil.

Mark gives me my tea in its perfect white mug and I sit at the table and my eyes feel hollow. I look at the brown liquid that's steaming and swirling from having all the teaspoons of teeth-rotting sugar stirred into it and I can't stop staring until the whirlpool is calm. He tells me Mum suddenly wasn't very well and that Rhoda and Max came

home on the bus and found her ill and now all these people are here because of that. I know she's had another seizure and I feel a bit better when I think that, because she's
always been all right after them. I ask if she's okay in a
voice that tears like tissue paper.

And then Mark sets down his own white mug and he
looks at me and he tells me he doesn't know.

And then the world stops spinning.

And then all the chaos rushes in.

7 15 14 5

I AM NOT the boy with the strange brother anymore. I
am not the boy who has magic soccer feet. I am not the
boy who can do math faster than the speed of light. I am
not the boy who's a bit too skinny. I am not the boy who
didn't fight Noah. I am not the boy who lives in a ramshackle house. I am not the boy who writes his feelings
and thoughts and memories in secret code. I am not the
boy who rides his bike too fast down hills and whoops at
all the people who watch the whizzing blur fly by them.

I am the boy whose mother died.

DAD COMES HOME from the hospital and he says *she looked very peaceful* but he says it in the way that people say things because that's what everyone has always said and so it sounds right. He puts his hands on my shoulders like Mark had done and it makes me feel like I have to be bigger and braver than I could ever imagine being. He tells me that Mum had been ill, a tumor inside her head but that this wasn't meant to happen, she was going to be fine, it was going to be fine, they were going to tell us when she was okay again.

She was having treatment at the hospital, a laser beam pointed straight inside her head and it was working. *It was working* he says and his voice is jagged. I think of all those slipped-out whispered visits in the summer when Granny M looked after us and she never said a word and I think of the haircut and the silk scarves that I thought were to stop Max's reaching fingers and I feel sick. *She said you boys had enough on your plates* he says and all his words have the trace of a sob etched in every syllable. He keeps saying *she was going to be fine* over and over and over until the words don't sound like words anymore and then Granny M takes my hand and gets me a Coke that I don't want while Dad rocks on his heels and cries.

Granny M strokes my cheek and tells me that *Mum's head started bleeding inside* and that *it was very quick* and that *no one could have known*. And I wish I'd known but at the same time I wish I hadn't and all I can imagine is a head full of blood, deep red swirling and crashing until there's nothing but darkness. Then Granny M says *no one could have known* again and again and it's as though everyone is stuck on repeat and I want to scream until it echoes too.

2 18 15 11 5 14

IT'S BEEN FOUR DAYS since Mum died.

Dad hasn't gone to work or emptied our trash cans or cooked our dinners or even had a shower. His eyes have sunk into his skull and he looks like a skeleton with a field of gray-splashed stubble creeping across his jaw. He doesn't cry in front of us today but the skin around his eyes is red and raw and always damp as if he's just stopped or he might just start. When I come down for breakfast he sits at the kitchen table and he stares into the space that we've all fallen into and he doesn't say a word.

I get myself some Cocoa Puffs and I get Max a bag of Quavers and make sure he sits at the table to eat them. Dad wears his ratty old bathrobe that Mum gave him a hundred years ago when they were still at school and Max and I were far away in the future. He hasn't even put clothes on when visitors come around and there have been a lot of visitors. Max hated it at first but now he just slinks down on the sofa like a worried cat and chews at the heel of his hand while the visitors put things like casseroles and stews in huge foil containers in our freezer. They make Dad tea and sweep away the undrunk cups that cover the table and wash them and stack them neatly in a perfect pile next to the sink as though they think that must have made things better.

I put my bowl in the sink and I'm about to leave it there but I stop and wash it up because my bowl from yesterday is still there and the Shredded Wheat crumbs have glued themselves to the spoon. I squeeze out too much liquid soap and the sink fills with bubbles and the bowl slips from my hand and smashes. Dad looks up as if he's heard something from far away and then carries on staring into space. I pick up the pieces of bowl and put them in the trash and then I sit on the sofa and cry.

Granny M comes over in the evening and empties the trash and puts a casserole in the oven because we'd just forget about it otherwise. Max will only eat bags of Quavers anyway. He won't have a bath which isn't new but he isn't having any baths at all which is definitely new. Granny M tries to coax him and she tries to tell him he can have special treats after his bath but she doesn't have what Max wants and he goes to his special book and riffles through the pages until he finds the little plastic cards that have all our family's names and pictures on them and he hands Granny M the card that says *Mummy* and my heart cracks and I think hers does too.

When it's time for his bed and his story and his sleep snuggles he stalks around the house looking for her and when he can't find her in the closet under the stairs or behind the curtains or in her bed then he opens his mouth and he howls. It comes deep from his belly and he's never made a sound like it before. It is a note of sadness that echoes through my bones and there's an ache inside me that feels like they're fracturing.

IT'S BEEN SIX DAYS since Mum died but I had to count because time feels like it's fallen apart. It's the day of her funeral but Max isn't coming because it will be too bright and too sad and too strange. It is too bright and too sad and too strange for me too. I wear a brand-new black suit that itches and that I will never wear again. The funeral is full of people saying *it was such a tragic loss* and *she was too young* and *what a shock* and did we *need anything* and all their words hum in the background.

Granny M takes me into the room where the funeral will happen so I can see the coffin. When I see it I feel my knees start to tremble and I have to hold Granny M's hand so hard that my knuckles turn white. I've never seen a coffin in real life before and it suddenly seems such a horrible idea to have a diamond-shaped box with a dead person inside it while all around it are the people they've left behind. I didn't see Mum after she died so I only have my imagination and it whirls and roars with images of her cold gray face stiff and lifeless. I put my hand on the smooth wood and I can't believe she's actually in there and I tap

dot-dot dot-dash-dot-dot dash-dot-dash-dash

And she'll never say it back.

Granny M cries all the way through the funeral because her daughter is dead and the tears cut crystal rivers down her cheeks but she doesn't make a sound. Dad cries too but he howls like Max and I don't do anything at all except stare at the wooden box and try not to imagine Mum in there. When the coffin disappears behind a curtain I reach out my hand and I can feel the crack opening up between us as she disappears forever to be turned back into star dust.

Afterward we have tiny sandwiches in a room that smells like the gym at school. Angelique is here and Natalie and Hazel and they never got to have that night out that they promised after Max said *dog*. Dad's parents aren't here, tucked up far away in Scotland. They said how sorry they were not to be able to make the journey and I was sad then but now that I'm here I don't want anyone to be here at all.

Dad's brother Simon leads him around the room like a tiny child and they get farther and farther away from me and I stand all alone. Mum's brother Dan squeezes my shoulder and tells me I'm brave and I don't know what to say because I'm not brave. I'm barely breathing and my chest feels bruised whenever I try. Dan gives me a glass of soda and I can tell he's trying to find some more words to say but no one knows what to say to the poor motherless boy so he just squeezes my shoulder again and drifts away.

Mark sees me standing on my own, frozen in space, and he wanders over but he doesn't talk either. It doesn't feel like he's desperately shaking his brain for the right words to fall out and he just sits with me while Dad zombie-walks from person to person and I don't feel so alone.

Some faces there feel familiar but I can't remember their names even after they come up and hug me and make my suit itch against me. Ahmed and Jamie are here with their parents and they're wearing suits too and it looks strange. They both give me hugs and it feels wrong because we never hug and I shrug them off and go and stand in the bathroom away from everything and everyone.

When I come back from the bathroom all people seem to do is chat and drink glasses of wine and some of them even laugh. I want to scream until my face is scarlet and I want to shout at them to stop and to remember that my mother is dead.

During the funeral Max stayed at home with Rhoda, who holds my hand between both of hers when we get home and then she pulls me into a fierce hug that knocks the tears out of me and I cry and cry and cry while she rocks me like a baby.

I know she'd been with Max when they'd gone into the too-quiet house when no one answered the door and she'd pushed the handle and found it unlocked like it nearly always was. She'd thought maybe Mum had forgotten the time and was out shopping even though that wasn't like her at all and then she saw a shape in the kitchen and she'd bundled Max back onto the bus even though that wasn't on his timetable and he screamed and thrashed and bit and then she went back in the house and dialed the emergency number and the whole street exploded into sirens. I know Rhoda had tried to help Mum because she knew First Aid and Granny M had called Rhoda a hero and somehow it felt true but it also felt wrong because Mum was still dead.

I take scissors to my suit that evening. I cut the jacket to inky shreds like the feathers of a crow and I think people might yell but Granny M just holds me tightly and Dad doesn't say a word because he doesn't know what to say and neither do I.

12 15 19 20

IT'S BEEN TEN DAYS since Mum died. Max goes back to school straight after the break because he needs his routine but I don't so I stay in bed. I want to hide in my attic space but I can't go up those stairs and into that room that used to be hers so I stay in my room and use my red notebook but instead of working on my family tree I write down words in code. Granny M gets Max ready that morning and he trots to his bus to see Rhoda and I wonder how much he even knows.

But when he gets home in the afternoon he scampers around looking for Mum and the next morning he charges into Mum and Dad's bedroom and he searches for her. I know now it wasn't his fault that Mum was so gray and tired and sick and I want to make it up to him, to whisper I'm sorry over and over and over and over again into the curve of his ear but I don't know how to start the words.

The next day when Angelique comes Max won't look at the picture cards. He turns his head away and when she offers him the spinning blue windmill without even asking for the card in exchange he won't take it. He clambers into her lap and he sits there still like a statue with his fingers tangled together and his eyes staring at something that isn't there while Angelique strokes his hair.

1 12 15 14 5

IT'S BEEN SEVENTEEN DAYS since Mum died. The air around me is empty and I haven't left the house since the funeral. Mark rings the doorbell at the same time every afternoon to ask if I'd like to walk Neil and at the same time every afternoon I don't go. Jamie and Ahmed knock after they've finished school and I don't want to see them because they're exactly the same and nothing else is. I sit in my room and I hold that glass paperweight we bought at the flea market and I gaze at the constellations on my walls and I try not to break into a thousand pieces.

19 9 12 5 14 20

IT'S BEEN TWENTY-THREE DAYS since Mum died and time is still broken. I haven't been back to school. Mrs. Havering sent one of the sympathy cards and now she sends work to me but I don't do it and Dad doesn't make me. He hasn't been back to work. He smells sour and he sits on the sofa in his bathrobe all day. The house is quiet and it feels frozen. I don't speak and Dad doesn't speak and the visitors start to drain away until it's just the three of us. Granny M starts to talk about me going back to school and I hear her say *Fred he needs to get back in his routine, he needs things to get back to normal* and Dad doesn't say anything but he's thinking the same as me that nothing will ever be normal again.

But the next day Granny M comes into my room and she throws back the curtains and lets the morning light drown my eyes. She lays out my uniform on the bed and tells me in a singsong voice that breakfast is waiting for me and I need to get up so I won't be late for school. I don't want to go and I can't go because I'll cry in front of everyone and if I leave this house then I'll come back and it'll still be empty and wrong. But Granny M cheerfully pulls my comforter off me and I move my limbs through syrup so that I'm standing upright. *Good boy* she says softly and strokes my cheek just like Mum used to do.

And so I go back to school and I don't say a word. Everyone comes to see me and their eyes are wide and Sam gives me his favorite Match Attax card and a girl I don't even know hugs me so tight that the air in my lungs pop.

At recess, all the soccer players get into huddles to talk tactics before kickoff and I follow like a robot. I am jostled and squeezed by the arms and elbows and shoulders holding me upright. I can barely breathe and I want to break out and sprint away across the playground and scale the metal fence and keep going until my muscles burn and my heart stops but I can't make my legs work.

Then the huddle breaks up and I haven't heard a word and I don't know the tactics. Everyone scatters to their positions but Noah stays right there beside me and he leans into my ear and he whispers *sorry to hear about your mum, Frank. Still, at least your brother won't even notice the difference, will he?* He says it so low that the words are almost carried away on the wind before they reach me but they do and they swirl through my ears and into my brain. And Noah walks away and shouts *on my head!* and the ball bounces over to him like a crashing meteor whirling through the blank space I'm in. All I can see is Max leaping through the house looking for her and howling his brokenboy howl because she's not there and I don't score a single goal and I don't say a single word.

I don't speak when Jamie comes around to play. I don't speak when Mrs. Havering asks me to answer a math question and then she thinks I don't know. I don't speak when Max pushes his thumbs into my eyes and the world explodes inside my lids. I don't speak when Granny M asks me if I'd like to go and choose a present for Angelique's birthday. I don't speak when Max melts all over the kitchen floor because the mugs on the shelf don't look the same as usual except they do to everyone else so we don't know how to fix it and he screams and screams and screams. I don't speak I don't speak I don't speak I don't speak I don't speak I don't speak except in my head where the words for what I am feeling scribble themselves again and again and again but I can't say them out loud.

I use codes instead of using my voice but no one can crack them.

dot-dot-dot dash-dash-dash dot-dot-dot

Mum would know, but she's not here to tap back. I'm not clever enough to make a code that sews the whole universe together but even the golden ratio doesn't give me a fizzing buzz anymore because Mum dying doesn't fit, it's not part of a perfect pattern. It doesn't make sense. I am scared of my silence because something is stuck in me like cotton candy in my teeth and I can't unstick it anymore and I can't make the words come out. Max doesn't like it because it's different and he puts his hands on my face and he squashes me and tries to squeeze my voice out.

19 15 18 47 44 23

IT'S BEEN TWENTY-EIGHT DAYS since Mum died. Granny M and Dad are having an argument in the kitchen and their voices are bouncing up through the ceiling into my room. I can hear snatches of fury and sorrow and I can hear Granny M's voice rising through the floorboards and seeping through the cracks and she says *she wouldn't want this for her boys, you have to stop you have to start looking after them* and I can hear Dad's sob-softened voice snaking up the stairs as he says *I can't do this without her, I can't do any of this without her, you just don't understand.*

I put my fingers in my ears just like Max does when he hears things he can't stand so I don't hear Max slip into my room and I don't realize it until he puts his skinny arms around my neck and buries his dirty face into my shoulder. He twirls his fingers in my hair and the crescent nails are black with dirt and he makes a low whimpering sound. I put my arms around him and I want to make it all okay and I say *it's okay* with my hands and I say *it's okay* with my broken, unused voice that unsticks itself in that moment. And even as I say it, I can hear Dad's voice rising again in furious waves against the floorboards.

Granny M goes to stay with her sister.

6   1   18   29   30   16   59   47   20

THAT WEEKEND DAD doesn't know what to do with Max and Max doesn't know what to do with Dad. They move around each other like wolves, circling and nervous. Dad tries to get Max to wear clothes and to eat food and to take a bath and to sit still, but Max doesn't want to do any of those things so he doesn't and he's gray and grubby and sad. Max is fading away and I don't know how to help him and I'm not sure if I have the energy inside me to try. I want Mum to come walking into the kitchen, smelling of cinnamon and sugar, and I want her to take Max by the hand and run him a color-streaked bubble bath and scrub away his grime and tears and then I want her to wrap us both up in thick blankets and sit next to us on the sofa while she tells us a story from inside her own head and draws the pictures to go with it. I want to cuddle into her soft warmth and I want it so badly that I can feel the ache in my chest like a bruise.

Max and Dad and I have fallen apart and there's no one to pick up the pieces and glue us back together again. Max spins further and further away from me and Dad is far away across the galaxy and I can't reach out and touch them.

18 15 1 13 9 14 7 29 23 38 12 4

IT'S BEEN THIRTY-FOUR DAYS since Mum died. The food in foil trays stops arriving and the cards stop coming through the door. The world spins on and we are trapped in the same space and the same place. My school uniform is always dirty and crumpled and when I try to use the washing machine I shrink my sweater. Dad goes back to work but he finishes early every day because he hasn't got anyone to be there when Max gets home from school. But Dad being there doesn't make a difference because Max just roams and Dad just lets him and even Angelique can't get Max to sit down and look at picture cards or toys with glitter spinning inside them. Granny M comes around but the creaks in her bones mean she can't help Max when he melts with a fury we've never seen before. He scribbles on the doors and rips pillows until there's feather snow tumbling through the air.

13 5 12 20 4 15 23 14

IT'S BEEN FORTY DAYS since Mum died. The casseroles and the stews are all gone and there's nothing in the fridge when I open it except an old dried lemon that is as light as air when I pick it up. The freezer has frozen over with ice and I imagine I'm an intrepid mountaineer chipping away at a sheer cliff face as I try to open it and see if there's anything at all for us to eat but there isn't and my hands go purple and Dad sees the ice storm on the floor. For a moment I think he'll yell but he just sits down on the sofa and rubs his hands across his sandpaper beard and Max hates the noise. I think Dad will stay slumped there for the rest of the evening and I'll eat cornflakes with no milk for dinner and pretend it's dehydrated space food.

But then he stands up and says *we need to go out and get some food.* There's no one to have Max while we go and I think *this isn't going to work* but when I say it Dad snaps at me and says that *Max'll just have to cope.* I wait for him to show Max the coat and shoes cards and the store card

but he doesn't and he starts to get the coats and shoes anyway and then I know it won't work.

I look through the plastic squares and I find the right
ones and I fumble and stick them onto the Velcro strip in
Max's special book and try to show them to Max but he's
not used to me doing it and he's not sure. I say *first coat then
shoes then store then cookie* and he pulls *cookie* off and gives
it to me. He's getting too clever for this and I don't know
what to do. **Come on Frank** shouts Dad and he doesn't
say it loudly in the way he would if he thought I might not
hear him. He shouts it like I'm doing something wrong and
Max screams and I swallow until my throat is dry.

Dad wrestles Max into the car and he wrestles him out
of the car and Max screams all the way there and he screams
all the way through the grocery store. The lights are too
bright and there's no list and Dad tries to put things in the
shopping cart and hold on to Max while he melts down and
down and down. Everyone looks at the wild-eyed bearded
man in crumpled clothes and the wild-eyed little boy with a
dirty face and a too-small stripy T-shirt with Quavers dust
sprinkling its seams and I try to disappear but they're looking at me too. Dad is trying to sing to Max in a raspy tune-
less voice and he's trying to tell him what's happening and
that we needed things like Quavers and other Max food and
things for my dinner and lunchbox but Max is far far away
and the words echo around the aisles and fade away.

19 16 1 18 11 48

IT'S BEEN FORTY-THREE DAYS since Mum died. Weekends are long and slow and painful and I keep myself curled up in my room reading my Superman comics from the flea market or playing Minecraft on the cracked iPad when it's not keeping Max quiet. But today I go to Ahmed's house for the first time since everything became empty even though Ahmed's mum was one of the people who brought food around and she always had a different comic for me and a little spinning toy for Max and I don't think I ever even said thank you.

Ahmed's house is different from Jamie's because Jamie only has one brother and their house is like Mark's with white walls and gray furniture and everything in its place. Mum said Jamie's house was beautiful and how isn't it wonderful that his parents were able to keep it so neat and clean with two children running around. We went there for Christmas drinks once and Mum kept Max in a grip like a vise because there were so many beautiful things for him to shake and drop and rip. Max kept reaching out for a teardrop-shaped glass filled with the flecks of a rainbow and so when he turned his head to look at the other treasures I moved it to a shelf and behind a picture of Jamie's mum and dad on their wedding day.

Jamie's mum kept laughing and saying *let him go, it doesn't matter* and so Mum released him while she had a cup of hot red spiced wine from a mug that was made of copper and didn't even have a handle. Max immediately pressed his fingers into the soft circle of a Very Expensive speaker and made a little mousehole. Mum went the same color as the wine in her handle-less mug and Jamie's mum said it was fine but it wasn't really because Max had broken something important and we didn't take him back again.

There are no expensive speakers or delicate drops of glass in Ahmed's house. It is very loud and full of people and squashy sofas and the walls are covered in bright pictures and draped with swirls of material. Someone is always shouting and someone is always laughing and someone is always cooking and everyone always wants to give Ahmed a hug or pinch his cheek even though he's ten. There's always so much going on that you can just blend into the noise and the movement and the whirling of people all around you and as soon as I step through the door I sink back into my old self just a little bit and leave the motherless boy at home in the quiet of our house.

Ahmed and I try to play video games but his little

cousins and nephews and nieces are there and they keep giggling and running across the room in front of the screen because they're playing some game involving imaginary crocodiles. And instead of getting cross and shouting at them like I would if Max was ruining my games, Ahmed throws himself on the ground and roars like he thinks a crocodile might roar and then he swims across the carpet. He snaps at their heels and thrashes his legs like a tail and the children jump up and down in a mix of fear and delight and a laugh escapes me and surprises us all.

I come home from Ahmed's with the laugh still fizzing a bit inside me like a tiny spark. I push open the door to my room and it's all wrong. I didn't remember to lock the padlock on my room with 0223 and no one remembered to do it for me. My soccer comforter is ripped and my Superman comics are torn into tiny little rainbow snowflakes on my floor. My soccer trophies are snapped and cracked and there are swipes of pen on my walls and my books are scattered in paper puddles. My books are my best thing because I breathe in the words that Mum used to read to me and they swirl in my head and I can click them together and pull them apart and make them sound just how she did and I can't breathe when I see what Max has done. Everything is ruined.

A sparkle of light catches my eye and sprinkled on the

carpet like shards of a rainbow is the glass from the paperweight orb that Mum bought me at the flea market. It was just right, it was perfect, it fit in and now it's broken and ruined and fractured and I let my feelings fly out of my mouth and I **roar.**

The roar is like something I've never heard from inside me and Dad runs in and stops in his tracks but I slip past him and I know where I'm going.

I thud down the stairs and reach into Max's special box where we keep all his treasures like his spinners and glittery balls and I pull out his stupid *Goodnight Moon* that he loves so much with its folded pages and crinkled spine. I tear at it but it's too hard so I stand on it and start to rip it that way and I use my teeth like a wildboy and I don't stop even when Dad comes in and wraps his arms around me and lifts me up and away with my legs kicking and I hold on to the book and when he tries to pull it from me it softly splits all along the middle and I don't stop until it's nothing and broken and ruined just like my room and now maybe Max'll understand.

And then I am shouting and Max is hopping through the house and his fingers twitch and shuffle and click for his book because he needs to thumb its pages and flick the corners and push his nose into the pictures so the ink smell flies into his brain and makes him smile. He hops and hops and hops and each hop is faster and more desperate until the rubber band inside him pings and snaps and Max is melting into fury and sobs and it's all my fault and I feel rockets launching in my stomach.

Dad pulls him tight in our bear hug. Dad tells him he's going to get him a new *Goodnight Moon* as soon as the bookstore opens tomorrow but Max isn't listening and he doesn't know when the store opens and he wants the same book that I shredded into a million angry pieces. And I want to scream and scream but Dad keeps his arms around us and holds us so close that I can feel his heart and my heart and Max's heart beating together in a drumming symphony. I try to struggle free but he keeps me close and I draw in huge juddery lungfuls of air until my muscles start to thaw and I feel myself relaxing into the warmth of his body and he keeps on holding me and we cry together and Dad says *oh my boys my boys* while Max runs his fingers along our tears.

That night Dad puts Max to bed with a story and the right way of tucking his comforter all around his little body. Then we tidy up my room together and Dad sweeps away the razor-sharp rainbow shards of glass. When everything is in plastic bags and I've got a different comforter on my bed, Dad tucks me in too and even though I'm ten, he reads me a story anyway.

The next day my uniform is washed and ironed and waiting for Monday.

6 15 18 5 19 20 48

IT'S BEEN FIFTY-TWO DAYS since Mum died and it's Christmastime everywhere but our house. Our classroom windows are iced with sprayed-on snow and there's a fat tree with spiky splayed branches in the auditorium. Year Six are allowed to decorate it and Mrs. Havering gets us all to help carry huge cardboard boxes overflowing with bright tinsel and glittering ornaments. I have been trying to ignore the lurching and whirling that gnaws in my stomach whenever I think about Christmas and New Year's Eve and all those empty years stretching ahead of me that'll put more and more space between me and Mum. I hang ornaments and I drape tinsel and I string lights and while I'm doing it I try my absolute very best to switch my brain off but it won't listen and it gets louder and louder until I go into the bathroom and switch on the hand dryer just to try to drown out the roar.

It's the last day of school before the Christmas break and when the bell rings out its goodbye I don't want to go home because this is the day Mum and I would go together and choose a Christmas tree. She would always want to get a straggly bedraggled one with brown needles and droopy branches that were already sweeping the floor. She said she felt sorry for those trees and they looked like they needed a loving home but I always wanted a fresh bright green tree that smelled like the Wilderness.

When I stomp into the house Dad is sitting at his computer and Max is holding a clear plastic snowman filled with little puffs of snowglitter. It's new and Dad says Rhoda gave it to him for Christmas and Max holds it out so I can look at the snowstorm trapped inside the plastic. I put the TV on too loud and Max clamps his hands over his ears and wails and his snowman rolls away from him. I click the volume up even higher to cover the sounds of his screams and I wish I could run up to the attic but I still can't go up there now because it was hers.

Dad looks up from his computer and says *Frank what are you doing you're upsetting him.* And I think **what about me what about me what about me?** and then the words fall out of my brain and into my mouth and I'm shouting.

Dad closes his laptop and he says *what's this all about?* and I let the words bubble out and I tell him about the tree.

Dad goes over to Mark's and when he comes back there are two sets of footsteps. Mark is in our front hall and Dad says *come on then, we've got ourselves a Max-sitter.*

Dad drives me to the place where Mum and I used to buy our tree and it's just us in the car and I can't remember that before. I put music on the radio and we sing along and we both sound terrible and that makes us laugh and sing louder and it sounds even worse.

There aren't that many trees left because we're so close to Christmas but there are still some that fill the air with the wildness of the woods. I wander around and try to choose one but not one of them feels right. Dad says *come on Frank, which one do you think?* And I keep walking through the forest until I get right to the very back where all the lonely brown trees are hiding and I say *these ones, these ones please.*

The man doesn't even want to sell us one brown Christmas tree and he says they're only good for the chipper and my heart lurches at the thought of them being chopped to smithereens and I say *please please please*. And he rolls his eyes and says we can just have them if we want and I look at Dad and he rolls his eyes too and it takes us forever to cram six trees into the car and when they're in there they look like all the colors of a bonfire.

At home I make a forest in our living room. Max isn't sure at first because this is new and it's not how it's supposed to look but I show him the color-changing lights and the glittery ornaments and he reaches out his hands to feel. I show Max how to loop the lights around and around the branches and hang the ornaments and soon the trees twinkle and throw rainbow shapes onto the walls.

On Christmas Day we sit in our forest and we miss her.

Then the fireworks boom and blast us into a whole new year and I feel like we're leaving her behind.

23 9 12 4 2 15 25 19

IT'S BEEN SIXTY-SEVEN DAYS since Mum died and on the last day before we go back to school after the holiday it snows. Thick and white and pillowy and it ices the houses and hangs heavy from tree branches. I want to take my sled with its horn and its lights to the Wilderness before it's dark. But it's only daylight for a flash and then dark licketysplit quick so going to the Wilderness will only last as long as it takes for the sun to drop and buttery melt into the sky. I go down the cold dark steps to the cellar and I drag the sled up from the damp spider-scuttling depths all by myself and then I call Jamie and Ahmed to come over.

Max sees me putting on my big coat and my thick hat and bright yellow gloves and he doesn't like it at all. Jamie and Ahmed look at the screamy boy stretching his hands out for me and Ahmed says *let's take Max with us*. And I don't feel that white-hot swish of anger and disappointment like I did when Mark said that all those months ago and I say *okay* and I get Max's cards to show him and I don't hide them from Ahmed and Jamie.

I pull Max to the Wilderness on my sled and he claps his hands and his face is split with a smile. Dad and Max have to come as a pair but Dad says he's not really there but he definitely is. He sits on a frozen tree stump and takes out a book to pretend to read while he watches Max in case he melts before the sun does.

Max is a jumping bean and he runs and whoops and tumbles down the twisty, snowy wilderness paths and I burn with worry and shame but Ahmed runs and whoops too and then Jamie and then I try it and I shout out all of the noises in my head and this is the wildest we've ever been and we are four wildboys in a wild wood. We make a racket and a din and Max doesn't push his fingers in his ears or bite his hands or smash his head on the frosty floor.

I put him in front of me on the sled and Ahmed gives us a shove and suddenly we are shooting down the snowy hillside, the sleek silver skis of my sled cutting perfect lines in the crunchy white beneath us. Max is whooping and he puts his hands over mine as I steer the sled to the bottom and we tumble off in a soft heap. We run back to the top and my mouth is stretched wide and I'm having fun with Max. I can see Dad sitting watching us on his tree stump and I can't be sure because he's a miniature man in the distance but I think I see him smiling too.

Our breath makes cold milky clouds in the air and we puff our cheeks and blow smoky streams because it makes

Max laugh and he huffs out his own air and catches it in his hands. Then Max holds out his hands for Ahmed and Jamie and I burn again because only babies hold hands but then they just take them and it's suddenly so simple. Max has no hands left so I hold Jamie's hand and we run down the hill in a string of arms and a tangle of legs and a burst of impossible happiness just for that sliver of a second.

When we get home Dad makes us all hot chocolate, even Max, and Max copies Jamie when he blows across the top of it to cool it down. He sticks his tongue into the brown milk and a look of pure shock flashes on his face but he doesn't melt. I don't say anything to Jamie and Ahmed about Max not ever drinking hot chocolate and Dad smiles at him and tells him he's a *good boy* and he does it with his voice and his hands. Dad sits with us at the table and he teaches us how to play a card game called blackjack. We use buttons to bet with while Max tongue-pokes his cooling drink. I get to use math and a bit of luck and I win the biggest pile of rainbow-colored buttons. Darkness is spilling through the kitchen window before it feels like something's missing again.

19 20 15 18 9 5 48

IT'S BEEN SIXTY-NINE DAYS since Mum died and we're back to school and working on our Big Project. It's the first lesson I've had on it since Mum died and I want to scream and scream that my family is ragged and torn apart. I think about the little cross next to a name that means someone has died and I think if I have to make those two simple marks next to Mum's name then I will die as well. I stare into space for the whole lesson and I don't let the nib of my pen touch the paper of my notebook. People keep looking at me sitting there, doing nothing, but I just keep blinking away the tears and Mrs. Havering doesn't come over and tell me to get on with my work.

When I'm changing in the cloakroom for PE I hear Lucy and Meggie whispering in the corridor that Mrs. Havering didn't make me do any work because my mother died and it would be *insensitive* to make me keep writing about families when I don't have a real one anymore. I swallow the hot lump of rage that rises in my throat and pull my PE T-shirt over my head. I think about the little books I made last term and my illustration that Jamie said was the best he'd seen. I think about the Family Forest that we're going to make and the cardboard and papier-mâché trees that will line the walls of the auditorium with the stories of all the normal families hanging from their branches.

I pull on my sneakers and then I creep back into the now-empty classroom. The playing field is filling up with my class, a scatter of PE T-shirts and the thump of soccer balls. I reach into my desk and I pull out the stories I've finished. I don't look at the picture of Mum and Dad and instead I shove them all deep into the bottom of the trash can underneath the pencil shavings and snack-time banana skins.

The next day Mrs. Havering makes me stay behind when the bell rings for recess. I stare straight over her shoulder out the window and I know I'm being rude but I know she's going to ask how I'm doing and if she can do anything and I know I might shout if she does that. But she doesn't. Instead she opens her desk drawer and nestled among red pens and rulers and half-open notebooks with important-looking writing scribbled on their lines are my family storybooks. I don't ask her how she found the books buried under the trash of a day. I look at Mrs. Havering and she's not saying anything and for a heart-lurching moment I think I'm in big trouble for throwing away my work and I can feel hot tears threatening to spill.

But Mrs. Havering doesn't shout. She doesn't tell me that throwing away my work was a bad thing to do and she doesn't tell me that I've got to pick up litter from now until the end of term. She tells me about her daughter.

Mrs. Havering only put her son, Jason, on the family tree that she sketched on the whiteboard all those months ago before the sky fell in. She didn't fill in the branch next to him because her daughter died before she was even born. *Stillborn* Mrs. Havering says and her voice jumps a little. Her name was Isabel and she was Jason's little sister. Mrs. Havering says she would be thirty-two now and that every year on her birthday she puts a spray of snowdrops on her grave and remembers her little life that never got to begin. And I remember Mrs. Havering telling us that *everyone has a story that's longer and more complex than we might ever imagine, even a tiny baby.* And now I know she was talking about Isabel.

Mrs. Havering says that she was wrong not to put Isabel on the tree because her life was important and it mattered and she would never forget her and neither would Jason or her husband or even Jason's wife and their children. They will all grow up with her and without her. And then she tells me that even though my heart must be breaking into a thousand million pieces I should tell the story of my mother and the story of my family.

THE NEXT WEEKEND I get up early. Mum's studio smells like mold and age and very faintly of something that makes my heart lurch. No one has been up here since she died. It's different now but it's just like I remembered, all at once. There are new tubes of paint and big tables and jars and brushes and some blank canvases with faint pencil lines scarring their skin. There are paintings leaning against the wall and I move them apart more carefully than I've ever moved anything ever and I see something half finished but completely us.

It's Mum, and Dad is standing behind her with his hands resting on her sloping shoulders. There's a little boy sitting on her lap, wearing a stripy T-shirt and holding something tight in his fist. And there's a bigger boy with curly hair standing next to her holding her hand and she's smiling like a whisper in the quietest, sweetest curve of lips and she shines from the canvas. There are patches where she hasn't painted in the color and the canvas is shock white where some of our skin should be but it doesn't matter one bit.

I breathe it all in and I feel like I can almost touch her. I look at the gentle curve of Mum's lips and the delicate tiredness that she's blushed under Dad's eyes and Max's skinny knees and my cheek pressed tight against her side holding my old red motorcycle in my other bony hand. Whatever Max is holding in his fist is just a sketchy outline and my T-shirt is just a white gap and Dad's hands are skeletal gray lines. I puzzle at the shape in Max's hand until I see the ridges and swirls of the ammonite I bought him from the Science Museum when I was in Year Five.

I stare at the blank unpainted space until my eyes blur but I can see it now. Penciled numbers strung together into codes, some peeping and spiraling out from behind paint, some stark and alone on the white canvas where I used to scribble my secret thoughts. Codes that unlock the swirl of feelings and memories I keep trapped in my chest and make them into something more magical. The canvas where I used to scribble my secret thoughts before she died.

I haven't been up here since weeks before she died. When she said she wanted to start painting again, she started with us. I can feel tears rippling at the edges of my eyes because she never got to finish it and now we'll never be complete. I pick up a pencil and with the lightest strokes possible I write all the codes I remember that I scrawled in the back of the red family-tree notebook instead.

I carry the painting downstairs just as the sun starts to push gently through the morning mist. I am so careful and I barely breathe as I hold it aloft and angle it so it doesn't bash into the banisters or the wall. I lean it against the hall table. Then I make some coffee using the special plunging pot that Dad always used to use on lazy Sunday mornings and that filled the house with something that smelled so delicious that I begged to try it and it was disgusting and I was disappointed and confused. It smelled rich and deep and so grown-up and it tasted bitter and like your mouth when you've just been sick. Mum thought that that was really funny but not as funny as the look on my face when I tried it and she asked me to try it again so she could take a picture. I look at the framed photo of me that is sitting on the mantelpiece and my eyes are crossed and my tongue is stuck out and you can almost hear me saying *yuck*.

I pour the hot water onto the coffee really carefully and then I take the whole thing next door. I have to leave it on the doorstep while I go and get the painting. It nearly blocks the whole of the doorway and I ring the bell.

21 14 9 22 5 18 19 34 29
48 11 25 58 77 16 1 3 63 87
32 15 106 13 44 135 116
7 30 12 59 24 54 145
164 20 88 47 193

MARK OPENS THE door and he's wearing pajamas and a bathrobe and his face is crumpled on one side and I think it must be very early. I think about turning around and scuttling back into my house but he smiles when he sees me and says *thank goodness you thought to bring coffee.*

Mark brings in the painting and rests it carefully against his sofa. He goes and puts on jeans and a sweater and then he sits at the kitchen table and pours the coffee into two of his white mugs. I blink away the images from that terrible afternoon and I sniff my coffee but I don't drink it. Mark says I'm probably a little young to drink coffee let alone enjoy it and he's trained himself to like it over many years. Then he fetches a bottle and stirs in milk and two fat lumps of brown sugar into my cup and it tastes a lot better than when I tried it before.

And even though Mark must know, I tell him about Mum and how she could paint the most terrible things, the most boring things, the most ugly things and she could turn them into something beautiful. I tell him about the smell of paint on her shirt and how the colors made the air taste. I tell him about the attic and the arrival of Max and the closed door and the dusty stairs and the way the paint faded from the air. I tell him about the screaming in the grocery store and what Noah said and Mrs. Havering's Isabel and the family stories. And I tell him my plan.

Mark stirs his coffee even though he hasn't put any milk or sugar in it. He takes a sip and he doesn't pull a face like I would. And he says *okay*.

I don't want to start small but Mark says we have to otherwise it'll go wrong because I won't know how to use the paint properly. *It's not like poster paint* he says and I need to know *what to do*. So he shows me. He takes me upstairs to his attic where the light is perfect and he shows me his studio. It is very different from the rest of his house. There's no white or gray or twisty bits of metal sculptures that look too delicate to breathe near up here. There's a shiny computer on a tiny desk and Mark says that's where he does his designing work, but that's not what I'm looking at. There are hundreds of jars half filled with water and tubes of paints squiggling across great big tables and brushes of every size sprouting from tins like flowers. There are big canvases with sweeping brushstrokes rippling across them and tiny canvases where the brush has just nibbled across the surface.

I pull out the two scraps of paper from my pocket and lay them side by side on a worktable. I *want to do this* I say. And Mark just nods again.

Mark shows me how to mix paints and tries to get me to copy so that I can get the colors I like. It's harder than it looks. I think that my plan might not be the best idea in the world. The names of the paints sound so strange and yet like I've always known them and I roll them around on my tongue. *CAD-mee-umm. OH-ker. Ah-LIZ-ar-in. Ul-tra mah-REEN.*

Mark says it's not a problem if the colors don't match his as long as I like them. He makes me write down how much I used of each color when I find a mixture I like and soon I have pages of torn paper covered with soft gray pencil scribbles.

Mark gives me a tiny canvas the size of a postcard. He shows me how to sketch out my drawing first so that I know where I have to paint and which lines to fill. This is just a practice so I sketch out Neil and then we find grays and blacks and whites to mix into the shades of his fur. Mark helps me with the brushstrokes and Neil's paint fur starts to look like his real fur and I can almost feel its wiry coarseness rising up from the canvas.

The next part is more difficult.

I have to go and get Max.

Max is up and eating Quavers in his spacepants and so I get him dressed as quickly as you can ever get Max dressed. Dad just sits on the sofa staring at the blank TV screen and he doesn't seem to notice us scampering around him or me chasing Max with a pair of pants.

Max loves Mark and he loves Neil but I don't have a picture card for next door and if I show him the card for Neil he'll think we're going for a walk. I load up the computer and click through until I find a picture card for *next door* which is just two doors with an arrow pointing to one of them and I don't think it's going to be very helpful. The printer whirrs and spits out the message for Max and I show it to him. He puts his head to one side like a curious baby bird and I take his hand and try to lead him out of the door but he starts to stiffen and his arms are flapping like a crow. His mouth opens and he shrieks and he drops to the floor into a puddle.

I go back next door and I tell Mark it won't work. He puts his head to one side just like Max and he's thinking and then he says *if Max won't come to the mountain then the mountain will come to Max* and I have no idea what he's talking about but then he grabs some huge bags and starts loading painting things into them and I think I get it.

I explain to Max what we are doing. He looks right at me and his dark eyes are like liquid pools that deepen as I speak. I want to hold him close to me then but I know he'd yelp so I just keep talking and he nods and his little hands flap but in the gentle way that means he's excited. And we bound up the stairs to Mum's studio.

We sketch together. Max and I draw the outlines of planets and the cosmos and swirling showers of comets and arcs of light that might be somewhere deep in space and pinprick dots of stars and Max is lying flat on the canvas Mark brought back over and his tongue is poking out in concentration and I've never seen him so still.

Mark helps us mix paints and choose brushes and cleans them when they get clumped with color.

We fill in the gaps.

We fill them with color and light and space and patterns and patchwork.

We paint nervously at first with little dabs and drips and then we make our marks stronger and bolder and the gaps close. I cover my codes with paint but I know they're there and they're nestled between then and now.

We fill our universe and our galaxy and our cosmos and our world with splashes and spots and streaks and strokes of paint. In the swirls of a galaxy I hide the dots and dashes that make up mine and Mum's secret Morse code message to each other. We make colors that are bright and deep and dark and dull and shining and we paint and paint until the whole of the canvas is teeming with the space we've made. It is one of the most beautiful things I have ever seen and Mark holds it up for us and we are lost in the depth of the universe.

It looks different.

It looks jumbled.

It looks just right.

Dad is still sitting on the sofa when we come downstairs and he's still watching a TV that isn't on. Mark tells him we have something to show him and Dad looks up like he's surprised that Mark is here even though Mark has made him three cups of tea today and said that he's looking after Max.

Max and I grab Dad's hands and they feel papery and dry but we pull him to his feet and we take him upstairs. When we get to the winding stairs that go all the way to the top of the house he stops and it's like there's a sheet of glass in front of him and he can't get through it. But Max shatters the glass with a yelp of excitement and we climb.

Mark has propped the painting up against the wall on top of one of the big tables. It's dark in the studio now and the painting is us and it's shining in the dim light. *We did it* I say to Dad. *We did it together for Mum.*

We weren't just her world but we were her universe and her space and her stars and her sky and her galaxy and her cosmos too whispers Dad and he wraps his arms around us and draws us to him and he doesn't let go for a long time and I can feel him crying but I'm not scared. Max and I have filled in the empty sketched spaces with all of the universe, together.

5   12   34   22   63   14

IT'S ONE HUNDRED AND NINETEEN DAYS since Mum died and this is harder even than Christmas because there are crocuses pushing their yellow heads through the dirt in the garden and Mum planted the bulbs when I was born. They're my birthday flowers and when I clicked my bedroom padlock shut today 0223 was true because today I am eleven.

Eleven should be the best age I've ever been because the numbers are the same whether you read them forward or backward and I've never had that before. But it doesn't feel right and there isn't the usual birthday spark of joy leaping in my stomach because Mum isn't here and she always made my favorite cinnamon cookies and my favorite chocolate cake and hung balloons from the ceiling where they couldn't rain down on Max and make him scream. We would have cake for breakfast and when I blew out the candles I'd close my eyes and make a wish and I burn when I think about the stupid things I used to want to come true. I'm in a whole new year and it's a whole new year that Mum doesn't exist in and it feels like she's falling behind.

When I go downstairs there's a funny rustling and I think Max must have got into the printer paper tray again and made snow. But when I go into the kitchen Dad is there and he's throwing streamers across the table and Granny M is there and she's wearing a pointy party hat and Max is grabbing handfuls of streamers and putting them where he thinks is best which is everywhere. And on the table along with the streamers is a chocolate cake and it's lopsided and the M&M's have started to slide off the icing but it's still my favorite.

They sing happy birthday quietly so Max doesn't shout and he signs *happy* at the end and we cheer for all the words he's slowly collecting. I want a cinnamon-sugar hug from Mum that creaks my bones but I swallow the feeling and Granny M gives me candy to take to school.

At school Jamie gives me a new soccer ball and Ahmed gives me a wrapped box and he says I can't open it until I get home and that it's from him and his mum and dad and all his brothers and sisters too. I give it a little shake and I can hear a rattle inside but I don't know what it could be and I'm itching to tear off the wrapping paper and find out.

At recess I get to be soccer captain because it's my birthday and I score four goals with my new ball and I run around the field like a wild thing and everyone mobs me because I'm the boy with the magic soccer feet.

When I get home we have lemonade in glass bottles with stripy straws and little cakes decorated with sugar soccer balls and Max touches his tongue to one quick as a flash. Granny M gives me new soccer shoes and a book about spies. I open the present from Angelique and she's given me a flashlight for adventuring in the Wilderness. Her mum has sent me a tiny skateboard that you skate on with just your fingers and she's even sent Max a present. It's a funny plastic telescope which shows a thousand different colors that change their pattern when you shake it. He gazes inside it and watches the shapes falling and melting and twisting into something new and it is his best present ever.

Mark comes around and gives me two huge books about space and I'm about to open Ahmed's present but Dad says *hold on* and then he disappears out of the room. When he comes back, he's holding a big box and he's wrapped it so badly that the birthday paper looks like it's been in a fight but it doesn't matter because I tear it off faster than a flash of light. It takes me a minute for my brain to work out what my eyes are seeing and when I do I whoop so loud Max jumps but he doesn't melt.

It's a brand-new computer. For me.

Dad comes over and he's moving a bit like he's embarrassed and he says *I thought I could teach you coding, like we always said, would you like that?* And it's what I've wanted since I was tiny and it's what he's always said he'll teach me and I'm excited and squirmy with a kind of sadness that always seems to sit right in my chest and blooms whenever anything happy happens.

And when I open the present from Ahmed's family, there's an actual real-life robot nestled in a bright blue box and I know Dad must have been talking to Ahmed's mum because you can use computer codes to make this robot dance and spin and run and talk and I can't wait and excitement rises up and leaps right to the ends of my fingers and the blooming sadness fades, just a little.

23 9 12 4

THE NEXT DAY I have a birthday party in the Wilderness. Granny M ties balloons to the trees and we wrap the Christmas tree lights into their branches and it looks magical. We have a barbecue even though it's February and there's frost in the air and we eat wildboy burgers and sausages and pretend they're rabbit.

Jamie and Ahmed come and bring their families and there are children everywhere. Angelique comes and Mark brings Neil who sits by the barbecue and waits for sausages. We run and we yell and we sail through the air on our rope swing and I paint my face with streaks of mud and there is a flicker of Frank the wildboy again. In a quiet corner near an oak tree Ahmed and Jamie and I scratch our numbers into the dirt and make a pact to be friends forever and beyond.

Max stands with Dad with half an eye on the burning embers in the barbecue and half an eye on the running and jumping blurs of limbs that go flying past him while we play tag. He's wearing big earphones that Angelique brought around months ago and he's only just decided they're okay to have clamped over his ears instead of his hands and they block the noises that make him melt. He's still twisty and anxious and after an hour he starts to pull at his lips and gnaw on his hand and before he can become a puddle Angelique takes him home.

We light a fire in a circle of stones and warm our hands by it as the stars start to blink and the day is dissolving. Granny M lights tiny candles inside lanterns and their glow makes our shadows loom and twist and we try to make shadow puppets but they all look like monsters with too many legs. Dad brings out a huge birthday cake with twelve silver candles because there's one for luck and everyone sings happy birthday but there's a voice missing and no one tells me to make a wish and I'm glad.

I am eleven and I am a flicker of a wildboy once again and I am one more year of age and one hundred and twenty days away from her.

The next day Mark and Neil and Max watch TV and Dad shows me a new language of numbers on the computer that can make my robot dance and it's more magical than the Wilderness in twilight.

23 9 12 4 29 20 8 38 14 7

IT'S BEEN ONE HUNDRED AND TWENTY-TWO
DAYS since Mum died. We have a letter from Max's
school. It isn't just a letter but an invitation to his school
play and it has words in it like *educational* and *enriching*
and *self-expression* and I ask Dad what that means. He
says *it's the way we act when we want to show others who
we are and what we're feeling* but that doesn't make sense
because Max always lets us know when he's happy or sad or
angry. When Max is happy then he *is* happy and he's nothing else besides. Every bit of his body flickers with sparks
of joy and he's everything that it means to be happy in that
moment, and when he's sad you can see misery pouring out
from every inch of him. When Max melts each grain of his
body feels his rigid hot anger like they're on fire and there's
no space for anything else. I don't know how pretending to
be somebody else in a play will help Max be himself.

I'm not sure why Max's school is doing a play at all
because plays have lines to learn and words to say and new
clothes to wear and all the things Max cannot do although

he does wear his starry school T-shirt now. Dad says a play *can be whatever it wants to be* and I don't understand what he means but I will go anyway because I want to see the spaceship school.

Max has brought home the picture book that will be his play and it's his new most favorite book of them all and I'm glad because I ripped up his *Goodnight Moon* and the new one we bought wasn't the same. The other children in his class will be Wild Things and he will be Max. He traces the pictures in the air again with a fingertip and then he traces his name too and a **M A X** is penned with fingers.

And six days later at Ahmed's birthday in the almost-spring-dusted shivery cold garden with the liquid inky dark all around him he burns a wobbly letter **M** into the night with a sparkler and Dad cries. So does Ahmed's mum, and Jamie and Ahmed and I whoop into the echoey sky.

The Max in the book wears a wolf suit and sails far away to the land of the Wild Things and they are terrifying and beautiful and monsters and kind and Book Max is a bit like them and a bit like a boy. Book Max is in a new land and the story says he's far away across the world from his home and he wants to go back and be loved and I think that's Real Boy Max sometimes and the more I turn the pages back and forth back and forth the more Book Max and Real Boy Max scribble over each other's lines.

Granny M makes Real Boy Max a Book Max wolf suit that's real too and it has a furry tail and clawed paws and pointy ears and he doesn't shout when she helps him put it on because he's read the outfit a thousand times and run his finger around its lines. He looks like Neil and he looks like Book Max and he looks like Real Boy Max and he scamper-trots around the kitchen with clattery paws. He won't take it off even at bedtime and he holds the tail in his hand while he sleeps in his forest room and his syrupy sleep heat sticks his hair to his wolf-hooded forehead.

I howl like a wolf when I see him in the morning. Max likes the howl and he pulls my hand until I do it again and he stares at me in his wolf suit with his boy eyes and then he howls too because it's a very Max-ish noise but it's the first time he's done the same sound as me.

Max is still a wolf when Angelique comes around and he shows her his book even though he's shown her before but this time he's showing her because he's Book Max today. Angelique is very pleased by this and she lets us howl in the kitchen and she even joins in and I laugh until my stomach aches with its happy balloon. And Max asks Angelique to read us the story when he hands over a plastic strip on which he's stuck two squares and one says *I want* and the other is a picture of a book.

2   5   19   20   29   15   6   58   1   12   41

IT'S ONE HUNDRED AND FORTY-THREE DAYS since
Mum died. Max's class is doing their play in the morning
because they won't like staying after school because that's
too different than usual. I think that means that I won't
be able to go but Dad calls Wolverton and talks to Mrs.
Havering and says he's taking me on an *educational trip*
but he doesn't say what. Dad says to me that Max will want
me there and that's that and I'm surprised but secretly
pleased too.

We take Granny M and Mark and Angelique and
Mark drives us in his car that has a roof that can fold down
when you touch a button. I touch the button quite a lot and
Dad tells me to stop it but Mark just laughs and says he
did exactly that when he first bought the car. Mark wanted
to come and see Max in his first real acting role and Max
definitely wanted Mark to come because Mark is one of his
best people.

The spaceship school is made of whiteness. The walls
are scrubbed-clean empty nothingy white white white. The

idea of Max with his stars and flashing squashy balls and light-up shoes and color-changing windmill and bouncing walk pops bright against the blank. In Wolverton the hallways are filled with scribbly Year One drawings and a patchwork of paintings paving a path to the classrooms. I feel like my eyes are squinting into sunlight until I find the darkened room. It is the same one from the pictures I saw long ago with spinning lights and liquid tubes of bubbles stretching to the ceiling.

Rainbows bounce off the walls and I stare and stare and stare at the shadows of fat globs of oil flicking the ceiling from a lamp in the corner and the swoosh of a twirling ball made from colored glass. It's magical like the pier at the beach and splashes of white leak through the door from outside and become something beautiful. Dad says *Frank hurry up* and I pull my eyes away from the streaks of sparks. *Hurry hurry hurry hop hop hop* says Dad just like Mum used to and we walk through the nothing hallways to the auditorium and to Max.

We all sit in a big white auditorium on rickety rackety plastic chairs that rock when I move and I think of the time I tumbled and my arm went crack. My arm is knitted and fixed now but Sam broke his arm again last week when he jumped off the playground equipment and the doctor said his bones weren't as strong as before so I try to stay statue still on my difficult chair.

We watch two plays and they're not the same as the plays at Wolverton. The first class we see isn't Max's class and the children are a tangle of dressed-up bears and trees and people. There are thirty children in my class at Wolverton and there are seven in this one and five adults who are also dressed up like part of the play. I try to imagine Mrs. Havering doing that and it's a strange thought and I can't shape the picture in my head.

The children tramp onstage and stomp through paper fields of grass and wear squeaky clean rain boots to squish-squash through painted cotton ball mud puddles. They are bigger than Max but they still flip-flap and bounce on the stage and some of them hold a grown-up's hand. Some of the trees have pressed themselves flat into the white wall at the back of stage with their branch arms low and their heads to the side and eyes screwed tight but peeping through just enough to watch the bear hunt.

The teacher reads the words so the play has no lines but a story anyway and another teacher plays a piano and some of the bears have electric machines with big round buttons and sounds recorded on them, and sometimes they press them and it's the perfect time and sometimes it's not but it still works. The mud sucks *shuck shuck shuck* at the rain boots and the grass swishes and then as a big surprise there's real water when a little boy with red hair uses a spray bottle to make the river splash. Rain falls on the audience and they clap but whisper-soft quietly so the bears and trees don't scream.

Then it's Max and no one reads the words because Max can tell this story all by himself even if he doesn't make a sound. I see him and I forget about my rickety chair and the white walls and misery and Mum and I just see Max. Max in his furry wolf suit. Max with his cardboard cutout boat with painty fingerprints walking down the side and his wobbly M A X signature sloping away from him where he's raced through the alphabet to find his own code. Max with his bouncing wolf lollop and clattery claws. Max with his beaming smile stretching out forever on the map of his face. Max with his clawpaw clasping his teacher's hand and then letting go and running free. Max is the only wolf boy on the stage and he twirls around his world finding Wild Things and sailing through ocean storms and rumpus dancing under an invisible starry sky until he wants to be somewhere where somebody loves him best of all and he takes a swooping bow and jumps off the stage and throws his arms around us.

After Max has clambered back onto the stage and sailed home in his boat and the Wild Things have roared and clawed and gnashed and one has laid down on the floor and maybe one has gone to sleep we all clap and the plays are over.

The head teacher stands on the stage but she doesn't talk forever and ever like Mrs. Owens at Wolverton. She is wearing blue jeans and a bright green top with tiny white splodges and when I squint I can see that the splodges are cats. She says her name is Kate and she's pleased we could all come and see such *magnificent performances*. I'm surprised she is wearing jeans because teachers at Wolverton aren't allowed to do that and I'm even more surprised she said her first name because everyone knows that teachers usually guard their first names with their lives. Then Kate says she particularly enjoyed Max's performance especially his *improvisation* and the audience does a little laugh and we all shuffle upright in our wonky chairs and are puffed out with pride.

Kate tells us we can go to the classrooms and have juice and cookies with the actors and when she says *actors* I think it sounds funny but then I think it's true. So it's back into the blank white hallways blending into a blurry tunnel.

Max's classroom is white too but the children in it are fireworks of color and movement and noise. They jump and leap and twirl and flap and bounce and play with their voices so they squeak and growl and shriek and sing. A boy smaller than Max is carefully balancing a plastic plate of cookies in his hands and his tongue is stuck out with effort and concentration so he keeps forgetting to offer them to the visitors, who are us. I finally get a chocolate cookie and I say *thank you* and then I remember and say *thank you* with my hands too and the little boy leaps up and down with jumping joy and I catch the falling cookies.

Max's teacher is named Georgia and he loves her. He flings his skinny arms around her before he sees we are there and he looks up at her with big eyes like Neil when you have a piece of cheese. Georgia says to him that *Angelique and Granny and Daddy and Frank are here* and then she sees Mark and he holds out his hand and says he's our friend and he is. Max does a spin and sees me eating a cookie and Mark and Angelique admiring a display board of finger-painted fish and Granny M and Dad holding plastic glasses of juice.

Max's face is crumply and he's twisty and cross because it's not the play anymore and he's in his classroom and this is wrong because we are home and this is school. Max's little hands start to flap down low and he *beep beep beeps* his voice as a warning. Georgia puts her hands on his sloping shoulders and grips them and then presses down hard and I think that she's being too strong and Max's skinny boy body will buckle and fall but he stands up tall as she squeezes and sings a quiet song. *It's different, it's strange, it's certainly a change, but there's no need to be afraid so be brave so be brave so be brave.* The words are softly low and I dip my head and catch them in my ears and I hum along with the tune because it's one everybody knows but I don't know how.

And Max is calm.

16 18 15 21 4

I HAVE TO go back to my school after Max's play and
Max's not-melting. The hallways and walls are messy and
familiar and I trudge back to learn about the Tudors for
four minutes before the lunch bell goes *brrrring* and our
flippy desks go *slam* and our feet *stomp* and it sounds like
music. Mrs. Havering shouts at us to walk not run but
we don't really listen and we scatter into the playground
to wait for Year Six's turn in the lunchroom. The soccer players start to divvy up teams and Sam shouts that
he'll be referee because it's the *official position of anyone
with a broken arm,* which has only been me and him
so far, so he doesn't really need to say it but Sam likes to
shout.

We are in our tight knots of teams talking tactics
because that's what the best players do. Noah is on our
team because Jamie and Ahmed weren't pickers today
and Kai was and Noah scores goals. Noah keeps shouting
slide tackle slide tackle slam their legs and I want him to
shut up shut up shut up. I stop listening until

Kai is bored with Noah yelling and asks me where I was all morning. I pause with a lie caught in my mouth and I swallow it back down and I can feel it sinking darkly and dissolving. I say *I watched my brother Max in his school play*. Noah pulls the face he thinks is like Max and he says *how can **that** even be in a play it can't even talk* and then he does his yelping laugh like the hyenas from cartoons.

Ahmed and Jamie clench their fists again but I just keep talking and talking and all the words and thoughts in my head spill out of my mouth and I listen to them for the first time. I say *he played Max and he went to the land of the Wild Things in his private boat with his very own name painted on it by Max and not a teacher* and then I tell them about Max leaping off the stage because he loves us best of all and Max writing his M in fire in the starry night and his first words and that he can speak in a thousand ways without words and he can show all the moments of his day in just his face, and his body talks in a way mine never can and he can be in a play and speak no words from his mouth and tell the whole story anyway and about him sledding down the Wilderness hillside with us and his impossible infectious happiness and his rushing anger when the world is not his own and the colors and the noises and the changes that seem to hurt like a million arrows and about the magic squeezing that calmed Max's raging fizzy body bees and head wasps and that Max is made of star dust and that I am proud.

He is Max and I am proud. I say it again. And again. And again.

And then I walk away.

20 15 7 5 49 8 34 18

IT HAS BEEN ONE HUNDRED AND FIFTY-FOUR DAYS since Mum died. It's the last day of the first whole term I've had without her. Tomorrow Ahmed and Jamie and I are going to the Wilderness and I've made a promise to teach them Morse code using my new flashlight to make long and short flashes for dashes and dots so we can share secret codes in the dark.

The Family Forest is dense with trees of all shapes and sizes. Some of them are flat paper stuck onto the walls and some of them are made from papier-mâché and they're 3-D and stand up by themselves. Some of them are made from cereal boxes and old mops and have leaves made from torn-up shopping bags and tinfoil and tissue paper whispering in a quiet breeze.

There are families milling around, walking through the woods and exclaiming when they see their own name or their photograph stuck on a book that hangs from a cardboard tree branch. Noah is keeping his head low and trudging behind his parents and I'm surprised to see him walking like that but his father strides ahead with a stony face like he doesn't want to be here at all. Jamie's mum is giving him a hug and all of Ahmed's family are crowded around his creation, which has candy wrappers glittering among the twigs like jewels.

My tree took me and Mark days and days. *It's modern art* he tells me. *It's a sculpture that belongs in a gallery. It's beautiful.* It's just like I knew it would be when I went to Mark's and showed him my two pictures side by side. Our tree has everything. The golden ratio and spiral galaxies. The hidden number-letter-spiral cipher. Dots and dashes. My favorite codes.

We have glued together my family. Paintbrushes and glittery windmills and books and Quavers bags and soccer balls and picture symbols and canvases with Max's drawings of Neil and codes scribbled on paper and postcards from Granny M's hometown and pictures of Mum and Dad when they were younger and older stuck to all sides of cardboard boxes that help build the trunk of the tree up and up. We had to build it right here in this auditorium because there's no way it would fit in our car and it definitely wouldn't fit in Mark's, even with the roof down.

We glued the objects together into spiraling branches and painted them with blues and blacks and stuck on pinprick stars made from potato chip bags and swirls of universe created from glittery water-wigglers. It's a spiral galaxy of a tree and Mark measured and remeasured and measured again to make sure it matched the measurements of the code to our universe. Our family, rippling out and reflecting the whole wide cosmos, and the whole wide cosmos reflecting our family.

Mrs. Havering let us stay at school extra late yesterday. She was finishing her own tree, hanging a book with the name *Isabel* written upon the cover in perfect curling script. Next to her name, hanging from a branch of the tree, where the cross should be, is a tiny silver heart. I made it for Mrs. Havering when I made mine for Mum, and she swept me into her arms in a hug so fierce that it cracked my bones and held me together.

The branches spread out and from them hang all of our stories. Max's has our best photograph stuck on the front, where he has his arms tightly wrapped around my waist and he's not looking at the camera but he's laughing at something that you can't see in the picture. I'm laughing too.

Resting against the trunk of the tree is our family portrait.

I can see Dad and Granny M walking toward me and between them gripping their hands tightly is Max. He isn't certain and he is looking out of the sides of his eyes but when he sees me his face splits into a grin and I say out loud

That's my brother.

12 15 22 5

I AM ELEVEN and Max is nearly six. I lie on the floor on my side with Max and Dad. Between us is Max's new favorite spinner which is a Ferris wheel made from glow sticks that I bought him from the biggest toy store in the world when Granny M and I went shopping. We spin it together with our fingers sometimes touching and catching as the wheel gets faster and faster and the colors whirl and blur. The flashes whip past my eyes and I blink the blotches away but Max keeps on staring at the wheel. At me. I make a whooshing noise and Max giggles and our fingers touch again as we whirl the wheel together. Sometimes I touch my nose and Max makes a *meep meep* noise like I taught him and we all laugh.

Jamie's brother and his dad play PlayStation with Jamie every Sunday night in a death-battle competition and they have a league table and everything. But Max and Dad and I lie on the floor and *meep* and spin and we walk Neil and we read Max's books and watch movies and we get cross and we don't speak and then we forget all about it all over again. Dad works from home for now and I help him sometimes and he's teaching me to write more new codes on my new computer. Max helps to make my robot spin and dance. Dad and I made a game that Max and I can play together and sometimes he wins and sometimes I do. It's not the same as Jamie but it's not that different and it's not anything less at all. We miss Mum but we aren't spinning away and apart into space anymore.

Max can be far away in a world all on his own and Max can be right here next to me and Max can be near and far in the same snapped-finger moment. I spin the wheel faster and faster as Max claps his hands and he is here today right now in this moment and I am with him so I can crack his codes and bring him back when he steps into his boat all alone and sails off to the Wild Things. I am his best of all and I am not the Frank who couldn't be brave to Noah and laughed with the boys in the park and I am not poor motherless Frank and I am not part of something falling apart. We are our own spiral galaxy and we are spinning out into the universe and we are made of star dust just like everyone else. The code that holds us together isn't a golden ratio or numbers or taps but it's something bigger and better and harder and more mysterious and beautiful. I reach out through the slowing spokes and touch Max's fingers on purpose this time. Mum was right forever ago when I was five and he was new and nobody knew.

I am Frank and he is Max.

He's my brother.

And it's you, Max, I love.

It would not be much of a universe if it were not home to the people you love.

—Stephen Hawking